monsoonbooks

PRINCESS PLAY

Barbara Ismail spent several years in Kelantan in the 1970s and '80s, living in Kampong Dusun and Pengkalan Cepa, studying Wayang Siam and the Kelantanese dialect. She holds a PhD in Anthropology from Yale University, and is originally from Brooklyn, New York.

Princess Play is the second in Barbara Ismail's series of Kain Songket Mysteries based in Kelantan. The first book in the series, *Shadow Play*, won Best Debut Novel at the 2012 SBPA Book Awards in Singapore and was shortlisted for the Popular–The Star Readers' Choice Awards 2013 in Malaysia.

For more information about the author and her books, visit *www.barbaraismail.com*.

Kain Songket Mysteries
(published and forthcoming)

Shadow Play

Princess Play

Songbird

Moon Kite

Western Chanting

Little Axe

PRINCESS PLAY

Volume II in the Kain Songket Mysteries Series

Barbara Ismail

monsoonbooks

Published in 2013
by Monsoon Books Pte Ltd
71 Ayer Rajah Crescent #01-01
Mediapolis Phase Ø, Singapore 139951
www.monsoonbooks.com.sg

First edition.

ISBN (paperback): 978-981-4423-42-7
ISBN (ebook): 978-981-4423-43-4

Cover design by Cover Kitchen.

National Library Board, Singapore Cataloguing-in-Publication Data
Ismail, Barbara.
Princess play / Barbara Ismail. – First edition. – Singapore : Monsoon Books, 2013.
pages cm. – (Kain songket mysteries ; volume 2)
ISBN : 978-981-4423-42-7 (paperback)

1. Murder – Fiction. 2. Women detectives – Fiction. 3. Ritual – Fiction. 4. Kelantan – History – 20th century. I. Title.

PS3609
813.6 -- dc23 OCN847822387

Printed in Singapore
16 15 14 13 1 2 3 4 5

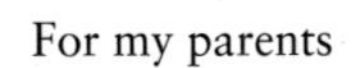

For my parents

Malay Glossary

Abang: Older Brother, a term of respect for someone somewhat older than you are. May also be used as a term of respect to a man roughly your same age.

Adik: Younger sibling, either male or female. Also, a wife.

Adik beradik: Brothers and sisters.

Alamak: An exclamation of surprise.

Alhamdullilah: Thank God.

Amok: A condition where brooding and anger result in unrestrained violence.

Astigfirullah: God forbid.

Ayah: Father.

Ayam Percik: Grilled chicken with coconut sauce and spices.

Baju Kurung: The traditional dress of a Malay woman consisting of a round-necked, long-sleeved blouse ending between the hips and the knees, with a sarong underneath.

Baju Melayu: Men's formal traditional wear: a high necked, long-sleeved cotton shirt worn over a sarong.

Batik: Wax print patterns on a cotton cloth. Also used as a generic for a woman's sarong.

Bersanding: The 'sitting-in-state' at a Malay wedding, where the bride and groom, in all their finery, sit on thrones.

Bidadari: Heavenly nymphs. Sometimes pronounced *bidandari*, combining the concept of midwife (*bidan*) with nymph.

Bomoh: A healer who uses both herbs and spells.

Budu: Fermented fish sauce, much esteemed in Kelantan.

Che: Short for *Enche*' (mister).

Cik: Miss.

Durian: A fruit with a thick, thorny rind and creamy interior, with a distinctive smell.

Enam Sembilan: Literally 'six nine'; a club made with rope wrapped around it, which leaves a distinctive braided mark, and is used, usually, on busybodies, to humiliate.

Hor: Kelantanese dialect for 'yes'.

Ikan Bilis: Anchovies

Jampi: Magic spell.

Kain Songket: The queen of Kelantan's textiles; made of silk with gold or silver geometric patterns woven into it.

Kakak: Older Sister, a term of respect for a woman somewhat older than you are. Also used as a term of respect for a woman roughly the same age.

Kampong: Village.

Kedai Runcit: General store: also a small stall selling necessities in a village.

Kenduri: Feast.

Keris: A wavy, bladed dagger; the traditional Malay weapon.

Kurang ajar: Insufficiently taught: rude and badly brought up.

Laksa (Laksa Kelantan): A popular dish with a thick curry sauce, usually with fish, vegetables and noodles. Every area has its own specialty; Kelantan's is the richest and sweetest.

Langsuir: A vampire like ghoul, the spirit of one who died during childbirth, which preys on pregnant women. It is usually seen in a tattered grave shroud.

Mak: Mother.

Mak Cik: Auntie, a polite form of address for an older woman.

Mak Su: An aunt who is the youngest in her birth family (from *bongsu*, youngest).

Mek: Young girl.

Nasi Dagang: Rice cooked with coconut milk and spices: a staple at Malay dinners.

Nasi Kerabu: Rice dyed blue, served with mint, basil, lemongrass, kaffir lime, torch ginger flower buds, raw vegetables, egg, grated coconut, chili paste and black pepper. Often sold as hawker food, wrapped in a banana leaf, and a popular lunch at schools.

Onde-Onde: Small cakes made of rice flour, coated with coconut, with Gula Melaka (palm sugar) in the middle.

Pak Cik: Uncle, a polite form of address to an older man.

Pak Long: An uncle who is the oldest in his birth family (from *sulong*, eldest).

Pasar: Market.

Pasar Besar: Main Market.

Pelesit: A familiar spirit, often kept in families for generations.

Perahu: Boat, like a fishing boat.

Rebab: A fiddle-like instrument played during Main Puteri.

Sarong: A tube of cloth reaching from waist to ankle: usually in batik patterns for women and plaids for men. The cloth is tied on the side for women and folded over the center for men, and is worn ubiquitously in Kelantan and other traditional areas of Malaysia.

Satay: A popular meal of grilled spice meat on skewers.

Sayang: Sweetheart.

Semangat: Life force, energy.

Silat: Malay Martial Arts.

Sireh: Betel nut.

Songkok: A Malay man's hat, brimless, usually of black velvet.

Tahi Itik: A kind of sweet cake native to Kelantan. The name means 'duck shit'.

Talak: A pronouncement of divorce. Three *talak* make a divorce final, and require another marriage before the two parties can remarry. One or two talak (they are cumulative) don't prohibit the parties from remarrying, and may be revoked.

Teh Beng: Iced tea served with sweetened condensed milk.

Tikar: A sleeping mat, used on the floor, usually of woven palm.

Tok Mindok: The leader or 'guide' during *main puteri*.

Malay Idioms

Air digenggam tak tiris

Water held in the fist will not leak: a miser

Anak baik, menantu molek

A good child and a pretty daughter in law: having everything one could want

Anjing galak, babi pun berani

The dogs are ready and the boar is brave: a fight where neither will back down

Ayam bertelor sebiji pecah khabar sebuah negeri

A chicken lays one egg and the whole country knows (as opposed to other creatures which may have large litters and keep quiet about it)

Bagai se ekur burong,mata lepas, badan terkurong

Like a bird in a cage, its body confined and only its eyes are free

Berteh dalam kuali

Popped rice in a cooking pot: constantly talking

Bukan harimau nak kerkah

He isn't a tiger who will chew you up

Cencaru makan petang

The horse mackerel feeds in the afternoon: said of people who take their time deciding what to do

Dapat pisang terkupas

Finding his bananas already peeled

Harimau menunjokkan belangnya

The tiger shows his stripes: you cannot escape your true nature

Hilang sepoh nampak senam

When the plating is gone you can see the metal underneath: to see someone's real character

Macam itik mendengarkan guntur

Like a duck listening to thunder: having no idea what you're seeing or doing

Masam muka macam nikah tak suka

As sour faced as an unwilling bride

Membeli kerbau ditengah padang

Buying a buffalo in the middle of the field: buying without looking (a pig in a poke)

Membuang garam kelaut

Throwing salt into the sea: a completely useless task

Pucat lesu macam ayam kena lengit

As pale as a chicken plagued with ticks

Pukul anak sindir menantu

To hit the child to get at the daughter in law: to do something to someone to get at someone else

Punggong dipukul gigi habis tanggal

To hit the behind and knock out the teeth: to do something to someone to get at someone else

Reba menantu api

The tinder awaits the fire: a fight waiting to happen

Salin tak tumpah

Not a drop spilled: a child who is the spit and image of its parent

Seperti anjing disua antan

Like a dog poked with a stick: snarling and ready to fight

Seperti gading dilarek

Like polished ivory: of a beautiful woman's skin

Seperti kucing dengan panggang

Like a cat and a roast: things which cannot be kept apart (like boys and girls)

Seperti lotong meniti dahan kayu

Like a monkey making his way across a tree branch: very carefully

Seperti polong kena sembur

Like a familiar spirit touched by water: furious

Susu didada tak dapat dielakkan

There is no avoiding mother's milk: you can't change your basic nature

Untong ada, tuah tidak

There is profit, not luck: to succeed by hard work alone

Untong sabat timbul, untong batu tenggelam

It is the fate of the husk to float, the fate of the stone to sink

Usul menunjokkan asal, bahasa menunjokkan banga

Character reveals origins, speech reveals breeding

Chapter I

Maryam could hear the drums thudding from across her village while she did the dinner dishes and knew soon enough that the chanting would begin. The patient in this exorcism, a woman of a certain age named Jamillah, worked in the main market near Maryam's stall, which is why there was a bond between them, of neighbours and businesswomen, though they were not close friends.

Jamillah was suffering from a variety of complaints, none of them serious on their own, but debilitating when put together. She was tired, she was occasionally vague and pessimistic, her arms ached and sometimes her back hurt. She was no longer the energetic and commanding *mak cik* she had been; several times Maryam noticed her stall had stayed boarded up during the business day, behaviour unbecoming any Kelantanese market woman.

Her grown children worriedly intervened, calling in a *bomoh,* a healer, to diagnose her illness, and – it was devoutly hoped – to cure it. He concluded, after due examination, that Jamillah was possessed by spirits who yearned to be understood and propitiated, and he wasted no time in arranging for a *main puteri*, Princess Play, an exorcism which would allow him to speak to the spirits involved, learn what they needed and then provide it, thereby freeing Jamillah from the lassitude enveloping her.

The drumming signalled the start of the ceremony, and the brushed and flattened dirt in the front yard of her house was becoming crowded with neighbours and family who travelled to show their support and concern. Jamilllah slumped spinelessly in the lap of her older brother, who struggled to keep her upright, while other relations sat next to him, sponging her face and encouraging her to take notice of the ceremony around her.

Her husband was nearby, staring dreamily at the ground while emphatically not taking part in the group hug going on nearby. However, from the gimlet looks he received from his two daughters, it did not seem likely he would continue in his isolation. In the general uproar, Jamillah was clearly the centre of attention and, just as clearly, he was not.

By the time Maryam and her husband Mamat ambled across Kampong Penambang, the *bomoh* had gone into trance and was in the possession of a princess spirit. In this state, he engaged in spirited repartee with one of his troupe to the amusement of the assembled crowd.

The ceremony combined healing and exorcism with general entertainment, and since the *bomoh*'s research into the case provided him with a wealth of information about *kampong* gossip, the spirits themselves were able to comment pointedly on local affairs.

Maryam took a seat among the women, next to her cousin

Rubiah, while Mamat wandered among the men smoking cigarettes and buying each other cups of coffee from an enterprising barista who had set up shop on the periphery of the performance.

Suddenly, Jamillah sat up straight, brushing off the hands of her relatives, raising her head high, her eyes flashing and alive, her expression imperious. She ordered the *bomoh* to account for himself in a voice not her own, and he bowed and scraped before her, offering a brief explanation of the problem as he saw it. In the background, the music continued, the drums joined by a flute and a fiddle.

Jamillah, laid low by aches, pains and exhaustion, barely able to keep her eyes open moments ago, now rose and danced in the traditional manner: fluid, graceful, full of energy and skill. Her daughters gasped, though they expected it as part of the *main puteri*. But seeing their mother move like a young dancer – confident, commanding – was astonishing, like seeing this most familiar of figures as a stranger.

The *bomoh* danced as her opposite, encouraging her first in this direction and then that, drawing her out in conversation. She gave her name as Mayang Puteh, a female spirit, and explained why she had invaded the body of Jamillah: to help her, to cure her, to encourage her spirit and life force, which was slowly draining away as Jamillah suffered, oppressed by evil, unable to rid herself of invasive spirits. She, Mayang Puteh, summoned by the entranced *bomoh* himself, would bolster Jamillah's flagging spirit, and drag her, if necessary, back to health. So she announced, as she glided effortlessly around the open space.

The appreciative murmurs of the crowd did not seem to

please her husband, now being prodded by his son to smile and nod. His sulkiness was noted by Jamillah's family, all of whom had heard about his recent lack of interest in her and her fear that he had turned his attentions to a younger woman. If that were the case, an accusation he strenuously denied, and for which even Jamillah could find no real evidence, then certainly he had not seen his wife as active and commanding as she was right now, the centre of attention and deservedly so. His children hoped this might change his perspective: his son encouraged him mightily to notice Jamillah and to admire her. The father smiled thinly, and nodded distractedly, watching his wife dance as she never had before.

The ceremony continued until nearly dawn – trance interspersed with comedy, dancing, singing and chanting, and Jamillah was the star. At the end, Mayang Puteh left Jamillah exhausted but exhilarated, cured of her symptoms, and buoyed by the Princess Play. Smiling, Jamillah staggered to her bed, from which she never rose again.

Chapter II

The Kota Bharu *pasar besar,* or main market, dominated the centre of town. It towered two stories high, with the cloth and produce sellers on the first floor as well as the building perimeter outside, while takeaway food and drinks were sold upstairs.

Maryam had inherited her cloth stall from her mother, who got prime territory when the building first opened, and she was in the middle of the market, on the widest lane winding through the stalls. She sold the pride of Kelantan, *kain songket,* fine silk woven with geometric designs in beaten gold thread.

Kampong Penambang was the hub of the *songket* trade and was littered with *songket* looms throughout. The main road from Kota Bharu to the beach, which also served as the village's main (and only paved) street, was dominated by imposing *songket* emporia, monuments to the *songket* trade, and Kampong Penambang's place in the centre of it.

Maryam was energetic and sturdy (as she liked to think of it). She had lovely eyes, large and liquid brown with long lashes, and a round and cheerful face with a small nose and full lips. Her hair was rarely seen at work, when it was bound in a cotton turban, almost always some shade of blue, her favourite colour. She wore, as did just about all of the women working at the market, a practical sarong covering her from waist to ankle and a long cotton shirt over it.

In the waist of her sarong, where it was tied, she kept a stash of home-rolled cigarettes, to which she often had recourse during the day. Mamat smoked Rothman's cigarettes, store-bought in a cardboard pack suitable for offering around in the coffee house, but Maryam didn't feel right spending so much on her own: she was comfortable with a more slapdash look to her tobacco.

In addition to *songket*, Maryam also sold cotton batik sarong, made by her brother Malek in his factory just down the road from where Maryam lived. She adored Malek with the enthusiasm of a little sister, which she maintained even in adulthood, and Malek, for his part, seemed to believe she was still eleven years old and was accordingly protective.

It amused Mamat to watch his otherwise completely take-charge wife defer to her older brother, and he in turn expressed concern as to whether Maryam should be coming home from the market alone after dark. Privately, he pitied any thief who tried to wrest her fabrics from her, but he amiably agreed to ferry his wife home every day, as he had always done.

Like Mamat himself, Malek cultivated a luxuriant moustache, which he stroked thoughtfully when he needed time to think. Maryam, of course, thought he was marvellously good-looking and didn't shrink from reminding her sister-in-law how very lucky she was. Malek's wife was a good-natured woman who usually, though not always, reacted with a smile to these pronouncements.

The morning after the exorcism, Maryam and Mamat piled folded lengths of *songket* carefully on the back of Mamat's motorcycle. As Maryam leaned over the side, adjusting the rope holding them in place, a commotion began across the village. She looked up in mild surprise: the *kampong* was usually quiet at this time of day, with people concentrating on getting to work or preparing breakfast rather than socializing. But this was not socializing either: the talk was strident and getting louder. Shooting Mamat a questioning look, she walked towards the activity, hearing snippets of conversation.

'Just like that ...'

'Last night, she was so happy ...'

'Not a mark on her ...'

Maryam picked up her pace, her heart now beating faster. Jamillah's oldest daughter, Zainab, pressed her hands over her temples and looked around wildly. 'It can't be,' she repeated.

'What is it?' Maryam asked to no one in particular, though she believed she now knew what she would hear.

'She's dead,' their nextdoor neighbour answered, looking confused, as though she couldn't understand what she herself was saying. 'I mean ... Aziz tried to wake her and she just ... didn't ...' She ended lamely: 'She must have died during the night.'

Maryam turned to Zainab. 'Nab, what happened?'

Zainab looked at her wide-eyed, her hair disordered and becoming more so with each movement of her hands, which she did not remove from her temples. 'I don't know, I don't know. She was fine going to sleep last night. Nothing happened. Then this morning ...' She bit her lip, unable to go on.

'Has someone gone for the police?' she asked gently, and Zainab nodded. 'My husband. I don't know why,' she added vaguely. 'Why the police? No one could have hurt her: we were all there!'

Maryam soothed her. 'Well, it's better to have them take a look. After all, it's unexpected, we should check ...'

Zainab's younger sister, Zaiton, came down the steps of the house, and put her arms around her older sister, resting her forehead on her shoulder. She said nothing: the two women held each other in silence. Maryam patted them on the back and looked around for their father. After a moment, she asked softly, 'Where is your *ayah*?'

Zaiton picked up her head to look at Maryam. 'In there,' she indicated the house with her chin. 'He's sitting with her.' Maryam nodded, and walked toward the house, leaving them to each other.

Her neighbours milled about at the bottom of the stairs, clearly unwilling to go up into the house, but feeling they ought to do something. Maryam nodded to one, indicating she would go inside, when a firm hand clamped onto her shoulder. It was her cousin Rubiah: her best friend and colleague.

'What happened?' Rubiah asked, guiding Maryam away from the house.

'She died.'

'Just like that?' Rubiah looked surprised.

'I guess,' Maryam answered doubtfully. 'I just heard. She didn't wake up this morning.'

'But last night ...' Rubiah trailed off. She looked a lot like Maryam, though her eyes were hidden now by her glasses. 'People don't die just like that.'

Maryam shrugged: it felt as though she was doing a lot of that right now. 'Zainab says they went to get the police.' Rubiah rolled her eyes; Maryam knew what she meant, but the police would just have to do.

'Don't look at me,' she insisted. 'I'm not getting involved here. I said never again!'

Rubiah nodded, and let out a long breath. 'Good, I just wanted to be sure.'

The police arrived in three cars, lights flashing, going slowly over the rutted dirt *kampong* roads. Kota Bharu's Chief of Police Osman thought, certainly not for the first time, that they would make a far more dashing entrance on a paved road, where they could come in fast and squeal the tires to a dramatic halt before the crime scene. But village roads required very careful driving if you didn't want to break an axle, and the painstaking avoidance of many holes required a crawl up to the scene, which was quite unsatisfying.

Police chief Osman stepped down from the car, and looked around the crowd. He caught Maryam's eye, and it appeared to her he sighed with relief, although he had no reason to, since she wouldn't be drawn into this case. Nevertheless, he passed her as he approached the house and motioned her to join him. She wouldn't help, of course, but was very curious about what had happened and, ignoring Rubiah's frown, followed him up the stairs.

It was still dark in the house; not all the shutters had been opened. No one was in the living room, though two *tikar*, sleeping mats, still lay on the floor. In the bedroom, Aziz sat on the bed next to Jamillah, silent and bent, her hand in his. Osman cleared his throat as he entered the room.

'I'm so sorry, *Pak Cik,*' he said quietly, walking to the other side of the bed. He bent over the body, looking at the neck and the wrists. Maryam craned her neck, to see it all. She could find no mark on the body at all, and nothing amiss on the bed.

'What happened?' he asked Aziz.

He shook his head pitifully. 'She just didn't wake up. She looked so good last night, so full of energy.'

'At the *main puteri*?' Osman asked, just to be sure.

Aziz nodded. 'Yes, she's been sick for a while. Very tired, not herself. But you should have seen her last night! Dancing! You saw it, right?' He turned to Maryam.

She agreed. 'She danced beautifully. And so much energy! You could see she was cured.'

'Could she have overdone it?' Osman asked, his eyes still on Jamillah. 'Maybe coming out of her illness ...?'

'I don't know,' Maryam said shortly.

'No!' Aziz's response surprised them. 'She didn't overdo it. I think someone killed her. She wasn't ready to die.'

If Jamillah had died during the night, surrounded by people, it seemed likely the first suspect would be the person sleeping next to her, who could do it (or something) without having to climb over anyone to get to her. And Aziz would be that suspect – so it seemed odd that he would be the one insisting on murder. Or was this a clever ploy to be first to mention what other people might be thinking in order to deflect suspicion from himself?

Osman reflected that he might have been in this job too long, already thinking like this in the presence of a bereaved widower, with his wife so recently gone.

'Look,' Aziz continued, pointing to her collarbone. 'There are marks.'

Osman and Maryam both leaned in, following his pointing finger. There were faint blue marks on her neck, which, if you looked at them a certain way, might have been from a hand. From another perspective, they didn't seem to be there at all. Maryam cocked her head in different directions while squinting, trying to bring the marks into some kind of pattern. But instead, they glided in and out of sight.

'*Pak Cik*, did you wake at all during the night?'

Aziz launched into an impassioned speech. 'I didn't wake up. We hardly had time to sleep by the time everything was over. She was tired, I could see that, but excited too. I was happy for her. I wanted her to be healthy, so I was relieved. I never expected ... well, who would ever expect? You never think, do you? My children are all here, it was crowded. Why would I think ...?' He stopped suddenly, as though a battery had gone dead, and looked at Osman, waiting for a reply.

Osman, however, had not yet mastered the Kelantan dialect, though he had lived in Kota Bharu nearly two years now. He was from Perak, on the west coast, and Kelantan's colourful dialect completely eluded him. It remained a real stumbling block in his investigative process, since it precluded him from conducting many interviews without the help of an interpreter. Aziz's tumble of words went right by him.

Maryam calmly gave him a synopsis of what had been said; the look on Aziz's face as he heard the translation spoke volumes on his opinion of Malay police officers who couldn't understand what other Malays were saying to them.

'Maybe ask a doctor to look at … her,' Maryam urged. 'Otherwise you'll never know whether there are marks or not. I certainly couldn't tell you.'

Osman nodded, touching Jamillah's wrist as though searching for a pulse. 'We'll need to know,' he agreed.

'Not we,' Maryam quickly corrected him. 'I'm not here. I can't do this again.'

Osman looked morose, but thought better of arguing. Now was not the time.

Chapter III

The doctor at Kota Bharu General Hospital duly opined that Jamillah probably died from asphyxiation. 'I don't think strangled,' he explained, 'because the prints are so faint. Strangling would have to exert far more strength. But she was kept from breathing.'

'A pillow, maybe?' Osman ventured. 'She was sleeping, so a pillow would be handy.'

The doctor agreed. 'It certainly could be. We could do tests to see, but the family would have to postpone the funeral.'

Osman winced. They were most anxious to have the ceremony take place the day after she died, according to Muslim custom, and Osman did not want to disappoint them.

Even if tests proved conclusively it was a pillow which killed her, would it change anything? She was dead: it looked as though someone had killed her while she slept in a house full of people. He gave a desultory wave at the doctor, signifying the tests were unnecessary, and walked into the hospital hallway where Jamillah's family waited. 'You can have the funeral tomorrow,' he informed Aziz.

'And my mother?' asked Zainab. 'How did she die?'

Osman considered how to say it gracefully. 'It looks as though she might have been smothered,' he stumbled. 'Asphyxiated.'

Zainab's eyes opened wide. 'No! How could that happen? We were all there! How could anyone get in?'

Her husband put his arm around her shoulder and drew her away from Osman. 'Wait!' she protested, over the growing noise of her relatives assimilating the information. 'I don't understand. How can it be?'

Osman tried to look calm and professional, but he had no real answer for her. *It was her husband who killed her* kept pounding through his mind. Who else could have gotten so close and not woken anyone else? But he had no proof, and no intention to hint at such as conclusion right now, though he shot a long look at Aziz, who looked straight back at him, expressionless.

He knows I know, thought Osman. It would be like a chess game, he thought, like the duel of wits he read about in the mysteries he devoured as a boy (and continued to do so even now), where the ace investigator and the criminal genius jousted, each anticipating the moves of the other. Justice always won in these contests, and Osman would not let down the side. He hoped Aziz knew what he would be up against.

Zainab still wanted to ask him how and why, but her husband and sister were trying hard to take her over to a side of the hall and calm her down. Osman went over to her as he prepared to leave, saying 'I will find who did this, and we will solve this. I can't answer your questions now, but I will, and shortly.'

She said nothing, but looked at him imploringly, her eyes glistening, as Osman made his way down the hall.

Maryam and Mamat went to the funeral, as had all of Kampong Penambang. Maryam felt the loss keenly: not only a fellow villager, but a colleague, another market woman. She felt a kinship with all her fellow *mak cik* supporting their families, and felt this as a blow to the whole sorority of small businesswomen. Rubiah, standing nearby, clearly shared her feelings, squeezing her arm as they helped in Jamillah's kitchen, serving the funeral lunch to all the men gathered in the front room. The daughters were understandably unable to organize, and their female neighbours took over the kitchen and the catering.

There was a low hum of conversation deploring Jamillah's death, and speculating on who caused it. The family said little, but news somehow leaked out about how she died, and everyone seemed to have an opinion on who was behind it. Naturally, since they were in Aziz's house, no one mentioned any theories placing him at the scene of the crime, but it was easy to read into the comments that he was a leading suspect.

Others plumped for a wandering stranger who had somehow climbed in the window, but most saw that for the polite evasion that it was. How convenient it would be to find that murder in Kampong Penambang was, thank God, the work of someone from far away!

Maryam and Rubiah ostentatiously concentrated entirely on preparing *nasi dagang*, the ultimate Kelantan celebratory food: rice with coconut milk served with *ayam percik*, grilled chicken with a coconut-ginger paste. As famed sleuths, they could not afford to give an opinion, which could be interpreted as based upon privileged police knowledge. Instead, they politely discouraged questions, stating simply they were not working in any way with the police on this case.

'We're through!' Rubiah insisted. 'Maryam was almost killed on the last case. No more!'

Earlier in the day, Maryam had said to Rubiah, 'You know know what Aziz looked like at the *main puteri*? *Masam muka macam nikah tak suka*: as sour-faced as an unwilling bride. He wasn't happy about it.'

But that was then, and here at the house, Maryam said nothing which could be interpreted as an opinion, and offered no expression which could be read to decipher what she was thinking.

Aziz sat surrounded by his family, expressionless, silent and alone among all the crowd. Maryam thought he looked separate from everyone, unconnected, while his children and their husbands and wives sat close together, the sisters holding hands. His isolation was self-inflicted: no one looked to ignore him, but neither was he at all approachable. Although Maryam believed him to have killed his wife, for reasons unknown, his isolation moved her to pity.

* * *

Two days later Osman appeared at Maryam's stall in the market. She sat on her stool of batik, a well-deserved cigarette between her lips and a glass of iced coffee and several cakes in front of her. Rubiah lounged in front of the stall, and Maryam looked pleased and cheerful.

'Osman!' she called to him, smiling widely. 'Come, have some coffee!'

Rubiah rose immediately to bring more coffee and cakes down from her stall upstairs. She was always gratified to feed Osman, who ate satisfying amounts of her cakes at almost every opportunity. He was so skinny! It was her own private challenge to bulk him up; though she thought that when he turned 40, he might start doing it on his own. Nevertheless, now it was her game, and she was going for a personal best.

'No, it isn't necessary, I've just eaten,' he began politely.

Rubiah snorted, having none of it. 'You just sit there,' she ordered him. 'I'll be right back.'

As she walked up the stairs, Maryam turned to him, 'Are you here for *songket*? I've just sold a whole wedding's worth!' No wonder she looked so delighted. 'Beautiful fabric, too,' she enthused. 'Cream. You should think about it, your wedding's coming up soon, isn't it? You can bring the *songket* back to Perak.'

'Well, my wife may want to choose it there.'

'Choose it there? When it comes from here? And you'll pay double for it? Really, Osman, what are you thinking? I'd be insulted if you weren't wearing my *songket*. I'll choose the very best for you.'

It was an order more than an offer, and Osman squirmed a bit, trying to find a compromise between Maryam's offer (very generous, it was true) to give him the fabric, and his wife's desire to choose her own for her wedding. Moreover, he hadn't come here for a conference on his wedding theme.

'*Mak Cik*,' he began, as Maryam examined the contents of the small box in which she kept her money, clearly admiring the amount now in there, 'I need your help.'

Her head snapped up to attention, her eyes narrowed, her lips pursed, and she held her cigarette between her thumb and forefinger. 'What?'

'I need your help,' he repeated, shuffling a little. 'I spoke to Aziz yesterday … and the family.'

'Go on,' she said shortly, seeing where this was going, but unwilling to join him there.

'He doesn't want to talk to me. He's very closed.'

'Do you understand him?'

'Yes.' Osman was wounded. 'I can understand him.' She looked at him unblinking. 'Sort of. The gist of it anyway,' he admitted. 'I had Rahman there.'

'Kind of awkward,' she commented.

'I think he'd feel more at ease with someone who wasn't official, someone he knows and trusts.'

'Really?' she said drily.

Rubiah arrived back carrying an oversized tray piled with Kelantanese rice cakes and a cup of coffee. 'What?' she asked, looking from one to the other, from Maryam's narrowed eyes to Osman's blushing. 'Oh no, not again,' she said to him. 'You're not asking ...'

'He is,' Maryam assured her.

'Eat this first,' Rubiah instructed him, putting a handful of his favourite *tahi itek* cakes on a plate and slapping it into his hand. She silently passed a plate of assorted cakes to Maryam, heavily populated by her own favourite, *onde-onde,* smaller and simpler than Osman's, but Rubiah found men tended to like the more elaborate styles. She was still working on why this was so.

'*Mak Cik*,' pleaded Osman, 'you know people open up to you. They talk to you, it's easy for them. You can find out things I never can. And you are so good at talking to people; a natural you might say. I need your help.' He looked morosely at his feet while eating a cake. It gave him time to think.

Maryam sighed. 'Osman, it isn't that we don't want to help. I'm just afraid. Yes! You don't believe it, but I was almost killed during that last case, and I don't think I could take it again. Besides,' she looked at him sternly, 'Rahman can handle it. He's very good.'

'Very!' Rubiah echoed.

Rahman was Osman's *de facto* deputy: a smart and energetic officer who had run down a suspect in downtown Kota Bharu the year before and had been badly injured in the process. He'd spent months recovering from a head wound and had to relearn many of his basic skills. Still, it had not affected either his intelligence or his willingness to work. Or translate.

'But Rahman is still not one hundred percent …'

'Neither am I after all that!'

'She's right,' Rubiah was indignant. 'Pushed in front of a car! How can you ask again?'

'Just talk to Aziz,' he pleaded. 'Just one conversation. I'll have someone there …'

'There? It's our own village! I don't need someone in my home! It's afterward, when they want to kill me.'

He sensed she might be weakening. 'Please!!' He gulped down two cakes in quick succession – from sheer nervousness, he told himself.

Maryam and Rubiah shared a look, and Rubiah rolled her eyes.

'Maybe.' Maryam said grudgingly. 'I'll think about it. I'll have to talk it over.' She gave him a dirty look and patted her money box. 'I was so happy this morning before I saw you.'

Chapter IV

Maryam and Rubiah stayed at the foot of the stairs leading to Jamillah's house. Unlike their previous forays into detecting, they wore no extra jewellery, nor had they broken out their fanciest clothing. They were just neighbours making a call after the funeral, to see if everything was alright. Rubiah carried a covered bowl with homemade *laksa Kelantan*, a noodle dish with thick, creamy coconut fish sauce. *Laksa* was a staple all over Malaysia, but every state had its own type; Kelantan's was the sweetest and thickest.

The elder daughter Zainab called them into the house. '*Mak Cik*, how nice to see you,' she said politely. 'You needn't have brought anything, so much trouble ...'

Maryam made noises to the effect that it was nothing, she was happy to bring it, and hoped they would like it. 'How have you all been?' she asked solicitously.

Zainab sighed, and signalled her school-aged daughter to bring some coffee. She leaned forward on the sofa.

'I miss my mother. It's such a shock. And to say she was murdered! I still can't understand that. How can it be?' she asked plaintively. 'We were all here, it was crowded. All of us couldn't have slept through someone walking in. It isn't possible.' She wrung her hands, and looked as though she might cry.

'Now,' soothed Rubiah, 'We must be brave. And look for justice.' Zainab stared at her. Rubiah then tried to explain.

'We're helping the police. You know, it's so much easier for neighbours to talk to neighbours instead of the police; they make us all uncomfortable, don't you think?' She smiled and nodded at Zainab, who hadn't so much as blinked. 'I think it makes such a difference talking just between ourselves.' She arranged her face in a pleasant expression and waited for Zainab to recover.

'Well, since you put it that way …'

'Yes, much pleasanter. You know, I had hoped to speak to your father.'

As if on cue, Aziz walked heavily into the living room where they sat, having just woken up.

'*Ayah,*' Zainab greeted him, '*Mak Cik* here has come to talk to us.' He grunted and collapsed into an armchair, raising his hand to have coffee delivered quickly. 'The police were here,' he said to Maryam.

'I always think it's easier to speak to your own people than the police,' Maryam offered. '*Kakak* Rubiah and I are working with the police, to help them, so to speak.'

He grunted again. 'Like you did before?'

Maryam shrugged and ducked her head. 'Like that.'

'What do you want to know?' The arrival of coffee and cakes seemed to cheer him and wake him up further. He looked at them alertly.

'Well, don't be shy! You're here to talk to me, go ahead.' He turned to Zainab. 'You don't have to stay if you don't want to,' he said gently. 'Not if you're going to be upset.'

Zainab sniffed and tried to smile. 'I'm alright.'

'Good!' Maryam began briskly. 'The night Jamillah died, when did you go to sleep?'

Aziz took a long sip of coffee, readying himself for his recital. 'You were there. You saw the ceremony. I don't think it ended until around two or so. Jamillah was exhausted, dancing all night. So much energy. Amazing.' He shook his head wonderingly. 'She went right to sleep, and I spoke to the *bomoh* for a while. And the family, of course. Everyone was staying here.'

'Where is he from?'

'The *bomoh*? Bacok, *Pak* Nik Lah. You know, *Pak* Awang here in Kampong Penambang said he was getting too old for *main puteri*. He told me about this other one. He was good, I thought. He came here a few times to talk to Jamillah, and to me, too, to find out what was wrong. Did a good job.'

'Peforming, you mean?'

'No, not just that. He did a lot of listening. You should talk to him: he probably knows more *kampong* gossip than I do.' Aziz leaned back and silently offered the women cigarettes from his pack. They all accepted and lit up.

'I think he tried.' Aziz was clearly working on articulating what he thought, 'Tried to get the background of what was bothering Jamillah. Not just waiting for *jinn,* you know, to speak up and tell him what's wrong. He looked at what happened to her, too.'

Maryam looked speculatively at Aziz. She would not have thought him a man to consider these things. He seemed so reasonable now, not the bottled-up man she saw at the ceremony. He cleared his throat.

'Jamillah, she hadn't been … happy. She was feeling sick, but she was also jittery. She thought I wasn't paying attention to her. She told everyone anyway, so, of course, I heard it. She thought I had another woman.'

He snorted and took a deep drag. 'I don't. I never did. I was worried, it's true, but there wasn't any woman involved.' He looked hard at Rubiah and Maryam. 'You probably think so too. It happens all the time, men my age looking for young women. I know that. But,' he stretched and rubbed his knees, 'not me.'

He smiled thinly. 'I have business problems. I didn't want to tell Jamillah.' His voice lowered, as though she might still overhear it. 'I didn't want to worry her. Maybe I should have.' He shrugged. 'It's too late now.'

'What kind of trouble?'

Aziz was uneasy. 'I don't think it has anything to do with this.'

'You don't know. It could have.'

He looked nervously at Zainab. 'Of course,' Maryam assured him, 'If you'd prefer to talk elsewhere …'

'*Ayah*, please. I'm a grown woman now, with kids of my own. You don't need to worry about me. We can help you!'

He cleared his throat again. 'I don't want this talked about. Nab, don't tell your *adik beradik,* it's really no big deal. *Ayam bertelor sebiji pecah khabar sebuah negeri,*' he mumbled: 'A chicken lays just one egg yet tells the whole country.'

He put out his cigarette and lit another one. He took a sip of coffee, and called to his granddaughter to top up their cups. He then appeared ready to begin.

Fixing his eyes on the window opposite, he said, 'I'm in business – or I was – with a ship's captain. Fishing boat from Pantai Cinta Berahi. I had a half share in the boat, it always made decent money. This captain, Murad, I knew him from long ago. I'm from Semut Api, you know, right there at Pantai Cinta Berahi. But Jamillah was from here, so I moved here. She was the youngest of her family, so she wanted to be close to her parents.

Anyway,' he brought himself back to the matter at hand, 'Murad wanted to sell the boat and retire. I thought I'd get my money out too, but then he sold it, or whatever it was he did, to his son, Kamal. I got hardly any money, he sold it so cheap.'

He looked at his cigarette, and though only recently lit, with an impatient shake, he stubbed it out and lit another one.

'You know, I can understand selling the boat cheap to your own son – of course, I can. But me, I don't have to do that. He should have bought me out first! He was always stingy and mean! But at least I thought he was honest. Now I know: *hilang sepoh nampak senam,* the plating is worn away and the real metal is seen. But it's too late, and I've lost it all.' He sighed, and ran his hand over his face.

Maryam made sympathetic noises. 'That's just terrible. And a friend, too!'

'No friend at all.'

'I know, but you thought … well, it seemed like it and now …'

'I've gone to talk to him, I've gone to fight with him. Imagine!

Two old men like us fighting on the sand. But I can't let it rest! *Reba menantu api:* the tinder awaits the fire. I will get back at him.' He looked grim.

'So Jamillah thought you had another woman?'

'I told her I didn't. This is eating me up. I wouldn't be surprised if Murad had something to do with it. Something to make me suffer, you know. *Pukul anak sindir menantu:* beat the daughter to get at the daughter-in-law. He could do this just to get at me.'

'Would he really go that far?'

'He could,' said Aziz stubbornly. 'He would, too. I'm sure of it.' He lit yet another cigarette, and passed his pack around. Zainab looked shaken, and her father tried to smile at her. 'Don't you start worrying too, Nab. It's alright.'

Maryam rose to leave, and thanked Aziz. 'We should be going now.'

'Will you talk to Murad? You should. You might think very differently if you actually meet him.'

Maryam was sure of it. 'We certainly will.'

Aziz looked troubled. 'Murad's sister lives in Kampong Tikat now. Maybe you should talk to her first, before you meet him. Noriah. Her husband is Musa.'

'Why?'

Aziz looked uncomfortable. 'Find out more about him before you see him. I'm telling you, he can be difficult.'

He nodded, and stood to escort them down the stairs, looking slightly, if not much more, relaxed than he had when they'd arrived. 'Thanks for the *laksa*!' he said as they walked slowly away.

Chapter V

Maryam squatted before a chopping board in her kitchen, while Rubiah sat on the steps pounding spices. Dinner waited for no one. Maryam's two youngest children, Aliza and Yi, both in secondary school, were already finished with homework and were planted in front of the television.

'He's acting differently than I thought he would,' Maryam advised Rubiah. 'I wonder about this Murad. Could he really be so bad?'

'I've never heard anyone pack so many sayings into a conversation,' Rubiah observed. 'More than our grandfather, and he was famous for it! I never knew them that well: do you think he talks like that all the time? Or were we just lucky?'

'It might have driven Jamillah crazy,' Maryam agreed. 'I like quoting as much as anyone, but really ...'

The onions and garlic were sizzling, and the chicken ready to be added. Maryam began grinding coconut for the milk

'We should meet this Noriah, although why we shouldn't go straight to Murad I can't imagine. Maybe it'll be useful.' She shrugged. 'Or not.' She was quiet for a moment.

'You know who I think we should talk to? The *bomoh* from Bacok. He probably knows a lot more about Jamillah than anyone else right now. I mean, he did all this talking to prepare for the *main puteri*.

Rubiah looked annoyed. 'I thought it was just this interview,' she objected. 'We weren't going to be part of the investigation, remember?'

'I'm curious,' Maryam replied, keeping her eyes carefully on the coconut so as not to meet Rubiah's. 'I know I said that, but now, there's so much more to learn.'

'I knew it. I really did. Even when you said it, I knew it.'

'Well, cheer up,' Maryam told her. 'Aren't you the least bit interested?'

Aliza suddenly appeared at the door, lounging against the jamb behind Rubiah. 'What have you found out, *Mak*?'

'You shouldn't get involved,' her mother informed her flatly.

'I'm not getting involved. I'm just asking. I'm curious.'

Maryam gave her a sardonic look and continued her conversation with Rubiah. 'So, Bacok tomorrow?'

'Are you afraid, *Mak*?' asked Aliza.

'Afraid?' Maryam scoffed. 'Why should I be?'

* * *

Pak Nik Lah lived in a sprawling 'urban' *kampong* right outside the centre of Bacok, a coastal town and district capital. Even with such a grand designation, its downtown was no more than two blocks long, and chickens wandered the scuffed lawn outside the police station.

Maryam and Rubiah stopped at a small stall selling a motley assortment of household necessities: *budu* (a much-loved local fish paste), matches, oil and salt. It all looked very haphazard, but there must have been some order to it, understood by its proprietor, a *mak cik* preparing coffee on a small gas burner. They hailed her, and she took the cigarette from between her lips and put her hands on her hips. 'Eh?' she asked, putting a complete questionnaire into that one syllable.

'Is the coffee ready?' Rubiah asked as one coffee stall owner to another.

'*Hor,*' the woman replied briefly; yes. Clearly, this was not a case of *berteh dalam kuali,* popped rice in a cooking pot, making incessant noise. She lifted an eyebrow to ask if they wanted any, and Rubiah nodded silently. The woman watched them with frank appraisal.

'We're from Kampong Penambang,' Maryam said, answering her unasked question. 'And we're here looking for *Pak* Nik Lah. The *bomoh*?'

The woman of few words nodded, but made no comment as to where he might be found. She simply poured their coffees into two cups, set them on the counter, whipped the dishcloth over her shoulder, and sat down, watching them. 'Are you looking to hire him?' she asked, finally.

'Maybe,' Maryam answered shortly. 'We just want to meet him now.'

'Oh.'

'Do you know where he lives?'

'Back there.' She jerked a thumb in the direction of a group of houses perched over the sandy soil. 'He's there.'

'Thank you.'

The woman lapsed back into silence, and watched them drink their coffee. When they paid and left, her eyes followed them all the way to the houses before she turned back to work.

Pak Nik Lah was a big, bluff man who looked as though he could pick up a full-grown patient and hold him over his head. He also had the professional ease of a *bomoh*, accustomed to handling difficult people in difficult situations.

He welcomed the two visitors into his house and had coffee in front of them before giving them an opportunity to state their business. He leaned across the low table and opened his large hands as if to envelop them. 'How can I help you?' he asked them, his eyes unthreatening but completely alert.

'*Pak* Nik Lah,' Maryam began, 'we are here to help the police.' He nodded as though this was something he heard all the time. 'We are investigating a murder: *Kak* Jamillah, from Kampong Penambang. You held a *main puteri* for her a few days ago.' He nodded again, and knit his brows.

'A real shame,' he pronounced sadly. 'I heard about it. Murder?'

'So it would seem. And we know, since you performed the *main puteri*, you must have spoken to many people about her.' As she paused for a moment, he nodded. 'I hoped you might tell me anything that might help us find her killer,' she said baldly.

He considered this. 'Are you really sure it was murder?'

'It seems so.'

'How was she ... killed?'

'It seems she was smothered. Maybe with a pillow.'

'In her own bed?' He was shocked.

Maryam nodded.

'But that's ... well, it's seems crazy, doesn't it?'

Maryam concurred; it seemed crazy to her, too. He shook his head. 'In her own bed? In her own house? How could that happen?'

'That's what we're trying to find out,' Rubiah interjected, tapping her cigarette against the ashtray for emphasis.

He leaned back against the cushion. 'I don't know. It doesn't seem possible even.' He looked at them both. 'I don't even know where to start.'

'Murad,' Maryam prompted him. 'Was he mentioned at all when you were looking into her problem?'

'Ah.' *Pak* Nik Lah took a long swig of coffee, and signalled his wife for refills. 'I'm not sure I should really talk about this. *Kak* Jamillah was a patient.'

'*Abang*, you can talk to us, two Kelantanese people just like you, who also knew Jamillah and want justice for her, or ...' she paused briefly, 'you can speak to the police. If you prefer that.' She looked at him demurely; she knew which she would pick.

He smiled ruefully. 'When you put it like that, *Kakak* ...' He thought for a moment, and then began to speak. 'You know, *Kak* Jamillah was worried, she was upset, and, of course, because of that, she was easy prey for *jinn*. An unquiet soul, this can lead to all kinds of problems because you can't defend yourself. You know, you're open to any kind of influence.

'She thought her husband no longer cared for her. He was moody and didn't pay any attention to things. I thought he was as troubled as she, but he kept it in more. Men do, I think.'

His audience nodded; it was well known. 'But I didn't feel as if he didn't care about his wife – I thought instead he had problems with someone else. And when I spoke to him about it, he told me about Murad and the boat. Have you heard?'

'He told us, too.'

'You see? It's preying on his mind. He can't think of anything else except how he's been wronged here. And it's turning his whole family upside down. Jamillah had no energy at all, *pucat lesu macam ayam kena lengit.* She was as pale and tired as a chicken plagued with ticks. But Aziz, he was *seperti anjing disua antan.* Like a dog poked with a stick. He was as sick as she, you know, but he didn't look as bad.'

'What did he tell you about Murad?'

Pak Nik Lah sighed. 'He hates him. He says he cheated him when the boat was sold. He was stingy, and mean, and supposedly kept a pelesit, which is how he got rich.'

'Is it true?'

'About the pelesit?' He shrugged. 'I don't know. I went to talk to this Murad. He is not a nice man. Not friendly, not warm. It was a very quick conversation, and when I talk to people about a sick person, one for whom we're planning a *main puteri*, people usually want to help as much as they can. They want the sick one to get well—doesn't everyone want to see a cure? Not this one.' He took a deep drag on his cigarette. 'He was angry that I dared to see him! Insulted me, called me a disgrace.'

'Do you think he killed Jamillah?'

'He's probably mean enough to have done it, but how could he get into the house like that? Did he send a pelesit? Maybe.'

Maryam was thoroughly unsatisfied with a supernatural answer, and refused to countenance some pelesit – familiar spirit—as a murderer, though she was reluctant to argue this point with a *bomoh*, who might well take it as a personal affront. 'Have you heard anything else?'

He cleared his throat. 'Well, Jamillah's younger daughter, Zaiton? I heard some talk about a marriage with Murad's son.'

Maryam opened her eyes wide. 'What?'

'Yes. Aziz wouldn't hear of it. Jamillah, I'm not sure how she felt. Zaiton herself might have had another opinion.'

'Might?'

'You should ask her.'

'Oh, I will,' Maryam assured him.

Chapter VI

For an interview with Murad's sister, informality was out. Gold was much on display: heavy earrings, a heavy necklace and several bangles glittered from behind Maryam's best head scarf. While *songket* would be overkill, the quality of the batik she wore was of the highest. They were dressed for combat.

Kampong Tikat was actually walking distance from Kampong Penambang, though it was a long walk along the main road. Maryam and Rubiah preferred it; it gave you time to think and plan what you wanted to say. Besides, Maryam liked admiring Kelantan's countryside and the lush greenery now that the planting season had begun. Rice paddies which had been just dry, cracked wastelands were now watered, with dark soil and bright green rice sprouts. It always raised her spirits to see the dry season end and the rains begin. Before the floods started, of course.

The large bend in the road signalled the boundary of Kampong Tikat, which also marked the gradual transformation from thick brown soil to sand: from villages devoted to farming to those of fishermen. Right there stood a long, large house whose porch looked out onto the main road. A young girl swept the front yard, keeping it a bare, flat expanse of dry earth, while two others hung laundry.

'Is this Musa's house?' Maryam asked pleasantly. The sweeper said yes, and smiled shyly.

'Are you his daughter?' she asked the girl. She nodded again.

'Is your mother home?'

She nodded once more and scampered up the steps, calling '*Mak*! Someone's here to see you!'

Moments later, a short, stocky woman bustled out from the house, looking like a general on campaign. She looked at Maryam and Rubiah with frank appraisal, taking in their bangles, necklaces and earrings in one glance and judging their value. Apparently they passed her test, for she ordered drinks and snacks to be delivered to her on the porch at once.

'Come up, come up,' she commanded them. 'Get out of the sun. It's too hot.' Maryam was confident she'd correctly assessed the right amount and quality of jewellery to wear, but validation was always appreciated.

'What can I do for you?' the lady of the house asked. 'By the way, I'm Noriah. And you?' She waved at the coffee, inviting them to drink.

'I'm Rubiah, and this is Maryam,' Rubiah began. 'We're here helping the police ...'

'I've heard of you!' Noriah exclaimed. 'You investigated that murder, didn't you? Well, you're here to look into another death, right? It must be Jamillah,' she guessed.

'I am,' Maryam was relieved to get right to the point. 'We're here to begin our investigation.'

'Here?' Noriah was surprised. 'Why not start at her home? Why would I know anything?'

'I was hoping you could give me some background first on your brother.'

'Ah, you've heard about Murad, then.' She smiled.

'Heard what?'

'Well,' Noriah reasoned, 'why are you starting here instead of just meeting him?' She lit a cigarette and passed the pack around. Not home-rolled, but store-bought. 'But you've heard he's a fierce one, likely to snap your head off. People are frightened of him.' She shrugged. 'No need to be. *Bukan harimau nak kerkah:* He isn't a tiger who wants to chew you up.'

'I'm not frightened,' Maryam answered mildly. 'I just didn't want to speak to him first.'

'He's a private man,' his sister pronounced. 'He's a fair man, and he works hard, that's all. Doesn't fool around much. He's always been that way, and it always made people think he was a little standoffish, you know. But he isn't, just serious and hardworking.' She leaned back against the wall of her house.

'People seem reluctant to talk about it.'

'And that's as it should be!' Noriah concluded. 'People shouldn't gossip; I think they respect Murad too much to talk about him. They look up to him,' she continued, sipping her coffee, 'they need someone to look up to. Villagers, I mean.'

We're all villagers here, all three of us, Maryam thought. *Who was she talking about?*

'The fishermen on his crew, for instance. These people need a leader, and I think Murad is just such a one.'

Maryam nodded silently, drawing on her cigarette. She let the quiet grow, waiting to see if Noriah would seek to fill it.

'If people fear him, it's because they are guilty themselves, and they think he'll discover their secret. You know about his fight with Jamillah's husband,' she guessed shrewdly. 'Someone who's innocent has nothing to fear from him.'

'Innocent of what?'

'Of anything! I'm saying he will see through you if you're a liar. Or a thief. But if you're a good person, he's kind and generous. But fair,' she amended, lest Maryam think he was simply open-handed. 'He's a fair man.'

'He was a ship's captain, wasn't he?'

'Yes. Have some cakes, please! You haven't touched anything. More coffee?'

They begged her not to trouble herself. They were fine – indeed, cool where they now sat – but Noriah followed the precepts of Malay courtesy, refilling their coffee cups and urging cookies and cigarettes upon them. They were profuse in their thanks.

'He was a ship's captain, your brother?' Maryam repeated after the flurry of politeness.

'He was. For a long time. He was thrifty and worked hard.' Thriftiness was not a virtue appreciated by most Malays; they perceived a short and slippery slope from frugal to downright stingy. Maryam was intrigued at the many ways Noriah inserted her brother's exemplary parsimony into the conversation.

'Did he start as a fisherman and work his way up?' Maryam was prepared to be impressed.

'Not really,' Noriah sniffed, 'our father owned the boat, and

Murad took it over. But there are plenty of men who would have lost it, you know. Spending money everywhere, mortgaging it,' her expression told Maryam this would count as a mortal sin in Noriah's world. 'Even drinking and fooling around. But not my brother. He kept the money he was given and made it grow.'

'Very impressive,' Maryam murmured.

'People here were suspicious of his accomplishments: but, as they say, *untung ada, tuah tidak:* there is success but not luck; it was all done with hard work. And therefore, they feared him.'

She took a ladylike sip of coffee and the merest nibble of a rice cake. 'He made plenty of money for Aziz, who didn't lift a finger. *Dapat pisang terkupas:* he had his bananas already peeled. He didn't do a thing.' This was not a compliment.

'And *Pak Cik* Murad's son now has the boat.'

'Why not? It's his son. A fair man, like his father, like his uncle, like his grandfather before him. He looks towards the future.' Maryam translated: doesn't spend money.

'He wants to have a family based on hard work and planning. To raise his children without spoiling them.' Maryam had never actually heard of this happening in any family she knew. People loved indulging small children. 'It's the right thing to pass on the business to a boy like that.'

Maryam smiled in agreement although it sounded cold and dull. Nothing like her own married daughter, whose husband adored her and whose small baby was treated like royalty everywhere she went.

'Now I'm afraid I must ask you some questions which might upset you.' Maryam began. 'Jamillah. She worked near me you know, in the market. Can you think of anyone who was angry at her?'

'Jamillah didn't make people angry with her.' Noriah stated flatly. 'She worked hard.' That again! 'And she was an honest businesswoman.'

Maryam moved closer. 'I don't know if what I heard is true, or just plain gossip.' She lowered her voice as though discussing a most sensitive secret. 'I understand there have been conversations about marriage.'

'Really?'

'Yes. Murad's son and Zaiton, Jamillah's daughter. It might be a good match. Is it true?'

Noriah gave her a very sharp look. 'I don't think so,' she said archly. 'Though my nephew will certainly make a wonderful husband. Zaiton would have been lucky.'

'I'm sure.'

Noriah bridled. 'I shouldn't think anything like that would happen. Jamillah was a reasonable woman, and one who recognized advantages! Aziz, ...' she waved her arm dismissively. 'But Zaiton had her eyes elsewhere.' She gave them a significant look.

'Another boy?' Maryam guessed.

She nodded, trying to look solemn. 'Not a great match, I'm afraid, but that's what happens when you let young people just choose whoever they want.'

'Who is it?'

She sniffed in disapproval. 'Someone who worked on Murad's boat. Rahim, that's his name. From Semut Api. Nothing in particular.'

'Is it serious?'

She shrugged. 'It could be. But now is not the time to talk of any of this. Not in a time of tragedy. Jamillah was a good woman.'

'Of course, she was!' Maryam agreed heartily. 'But sometimes people can become angry or resentful, through no fault of our own.'

'I think if you live correctly, you can avoid that. We are responsible for our own actions.'

'I wouldn't like to say that, *Mak Cik*.' Maryam was becoming annoyed. 'After all, someone did kill Jamillah, and I can't believe it would be her fault. How could it be?'

'I must say, my husband and I have been thinking what she could have done to bring this on herself. And I can't think of anything. She ran proper businesses, and kept herself to herself.'

'She was very nice and friendly at the market,' Maryam remarked. 'Everyone liked her.'

Noriah's face clouded. 'A person's life is not judged by how many people at the market like them. Nor will Jamillah be judged by that.'

Rubiah had been silent up to now, but could no longer remain so.

'Of course, it is! We're judged by how good we are, and that leads to people liking us. That's not what life is like here: fair, frugal, proper. It's more than that, and also,' she was gathering a head of steam, 'it doesn't have to be her fault she got killed. It could be the killer's fault. It *is* the killer's fault.'

Maryam was in no mood for a theological discussion. 'Please,

please,' she begged, spreading her arms wide as if to encompass both Rubiah and Noriah. 'Let's stay on this topic alone. I really need your help,' she gave Noriah her most imploring look. 'Do you know anyone, anyone at all who might have borne a grudge against her?'

She shook her head. 'Jamillah, no. Aziz, yes! But not her.' With this remark, Maryam looked inquiringly at Noriah.

'Well, Aziz could be difficult! We grew up together, my brother, Aziz and I, in Semut Api. Aziz got an idea into his head, somehow, that Murad cheated him when he sold the boat.' She laughed artificially.

'Nothing could be further from the truth! The very idea is absurd. But you know, Aziz just wouldn't let it go.' She shook her head slowly, and tried to look mournful about human nature, but Maryam thought she detected a gleam of satisfaction in recounting human foibles. 'Selfish he was, begrudging Kamal the boat. Murad was right to be angry with him.'

'Of course he was!' Maryam heartily agreed, while Rubiah regarded her with disapproving eyes. Maryam slid her own eyes away from her cousin, and kept smiling, hoping to encourge Noriah's confidences

Chapter VII

Maryam soon found herself back in Semut Api with Rubiah, wandering down the main road, now blown over with sand, looking for Rahim. 'Who do you think it is?' she asked Rubiah for the tenth time. 'She sure doesn't like him.'

Rubiah was not taken with Noriah. 'She doesn't like anybody. All that talk about fair and thrifty. What she means is mean and stingy. *Air digenggam tak tiris!* Even water held in his hand doesn't leak! And talking about it as though it were something great.'

Rubiah sniffed. 'We aren't people like that. We're generous and friendly. She doesn't know what it is to be Malay!' she announced triumphantly, writing off Noriah and all her pronouncements.

'It sounds miserable, all this fairness and carefulness and not spoiling kids.' She shook her head vehemently. 'I hope I like some of the other people we find a little more.'

'It's a murder investigation, after all,' Maryam reminded her. 'It might be better if we don't like the people we talk to. That way, you don't feel bad if one of them turns out to be the killer.'

She located a *kedai runcit* by the side of the road: an open hut nearly falling in on itself, with some forlorn bottles of kerosene, chili sauce and *budu* on spavined shelves. An older man sat behind his cracked counter, out of the sun, dozing.

'*Pak Cik*!' Maryam startled him out of his daze. He didn't get up, but raised his eyebrows to signify he was ready to do business. '*Pak Cik*, sorry to bother you,' Maryam smiled graciously. 'We're looking for Rahim.'

The man grunted, which Maryam took to mean 'of course'.

'Rahim, yes. He's working down at the beach. You can find him there.' As soon as he'd finished speaking, he shut his eyes; the store was now closed again.

'Thank you,' Maryam said. He nodded without opening his eyes.

The beach was only a few steps away. It was a wide swath of immaculate white sand dotted with gracefully bending coconut palms, leading down to clear blue water. Only the foam flying a few yards out gave hints of the strong undercurrents and riptides for which this beach was famous. The fishing *perahu*, the swift, single-outrigger sailboats, were still out, and the sun was fierce, reflecting off the sand in almost blinding light. One colourful boat was pulled up on the beach, and a few men were repairing it, keeping carefully in its shadow.

Maryam shielded her eyes and walked over to them. 'Rahim?' she asked tentatively. One of the young men turned around and stood.

'Yes, *Mak Cik*. Are you looking for me?' He was tall and thin, burned dark by the sun, and squinting. He looked friendly.

'Would you mind if I spoke to you?'

'No; but what's it about?'

Maryam looked around helplessly. 'Can we sit over there, under the trees? I can't even see in this sun.'

He laughed and led the way back to the trees, where they could sit in the shade. 'Would you like me to get some iced coffee?' he asked, starting to walk back to the same sleeping man they'd spoken to earlier. 'Be right back.'

He sauntered back in a few moments, while Rubiah was still mopping her face. 'Did you get this over there?' she indicated the *kedai runcit* and its sleeping proprietor.

He laughed. 'I know, it doesn't look like he does anything, but here you are!' He handed each of them a plastic bag with iced milky coffee, keeping one for himself, and lighting up a cigarette. Maryam promptly passed out her own.

'Thank you,' she said in heartfelt gratitude for something cold. 'How do you work out there?'

'It's hot,' he nodded. 'What can you do? It's a job.' He looked at them expectantly.

She introduced them both. 'I'm *Mak Cik* Maryam, and this is *Mak Cik* Rubiah. We're investigating a murder, helping the police.'

'*Mak Cik* Jamillah?'

'Yes, that's it.'

'Very sad.'

'Do you know the family well?'

He shrugged noncommittally. 'Any of them?' Maryam prodded.

'I know Zaiton; of course, I do,' Rahim admitted. He began to blush to the tips of his ears; it looked almost painful. 'But if what you're saying is that something ... happened, it didn't. Nothing. I mean, of course, her mother would want someone with more money than I have ...'

Maryam looked keenly at him. 'Her mother?'

'Well,' he floundered, 'yes, *Mak Cik* Jamillah, she would want a wealthier man ... But there's nothing to discuss here ...'

'And her father?'

He was silent.

'*Pak Cik* Aziz?' she reminded him.

'I know him better, of course. He owned part of the boat I worked on. I like him.'

'But he wasn't looking for a richer man?'

'I don't know.'

'*Pak Cik* Murad's son?'

He choked. 'He wouldn't want him,' he blurted out. 'He didn't like the family much.'

'But *Mak Cik* Jamillah did,' she prodded.

'I don't know.' He looked at her. 'I didn't mean anyone in particular.'

'Do you think,' she said kindly, 'that *Pak Cik* Aziz may have agreed to your marriage?'

He mumbled something to his feet, as he stared at them.

'And he still could,' she added softly. 'I mean, it still could happen, right?' He was silent.

'Come now,' Maryam said, encouraging him. 'We're done now. It wasn't so bad, was it?'

His look said it might have been. He stood up to return to work.

'Thank you very much,' Maryam really meant it. She liked him; he looked like a good boy. He smiled sadly and walked back into the sun, the waves of heat rising around him.

* * *

'I liked the boy,' Maryam declared to Rubiah on the porch after dinner. 'I don't want it to be him. But it could be a motive. After all, now, with Jamillah gone, Aziz might well agree to a marriage for Zaiton. In the light of day like this, it may sound silly, but we both know that falling in love ... well, it could do it.'

'He seems like such a nice boy!' Rubiah remonstrated. 'I just don't see it.'

'Was he at the ceremony?' Maryam mused. 'Zaiton would know.'

'Aliza!' she called, and her daughter materialized surprisingly quickly; listening from behind the door, Maryam suspected.

'Do you still want to help?' Aliza nodded eagerly. 'Go ask Zaiton if Rahim was at the *main puteri*.' Aliza nodded and started across the *kampong*. 'Wait!' Maryam called. 'Have you heard anything?'

'Heard what?'

'Any gossip about Zaiton. Any of the girls talking?'

Aliza wiggled uncomfortably. 'Sometimes, maybe ...'

'Aliza, this is a criminal investigation. No maybes.'

'There's a boy she likes.'

'Here?'

Aliza shook her head.

'Semut Api?'

'Yes.'

'Why didn't you tell me?'

'You didn't ask me!'

Maryam sighed in frustration. 'I'm asking you now. If you want to help, tell me!'

Aliza looked pained. 'Well, I don't really know that much. But there's a boy in Semut Api who's on her father's boat, and he likes her, and his family asked to marry her.'

'It's gone as far as that?'

'Yup. They say *Pak Cik* Aziz likes him, but *Mak Cik* Jamillah didn't.'

'Really?' said Rubiah, thoughtfully. 'Have they replied yet?'

'Not yet.' Now Aliza was entering into the spirit of the conversation.

'They were still talking about it. Zaiton wanted them to say yes. But her mother thought he was poor.'

'He *is* poor,' her mother pointed out.

'Yes, but they're in love!'

Maryam and Rubiah exchanged a telling look. No mother in Kampong Penambang wanted to hear that! Poor Jamillah must have been worried sick.

'Has she been meeting him secretly?' Maryam asked sternly. That would drive any mother crazy.

'I'm not sure.' Maryam said nothing in reply, but stared steadily at her daughter.

'Maybe,' Aliza admitted. 'I don't really know.'

'Go and find out.' She dismissed her. 'Did he come to the

ceremony?'

Rubiah shook her head regretfully. '*Seperti kucing dengan panggang:* like a cat and a roast. Boys and girls: you can't keep them apart. It's about time Zaiton got married.'

Maryam agreed. She said casually, 'You know, I've been thinking it's time Azmi got married too.'

Azmi was her son in the army, currently stationed in the south of Kelantan at Kok Lanas. He'd been living away from home for nearly two years now, and, of course, was a grown man, at least by his own reckoning, if not his parents' reckoning. Maryam considered finding a bride for Azmi before some girl found him – some girl who might not be from Kelantan, or even Malay.

Still, this news came as some surprise to Rubiah. 'Azmi?' she asked. 'Have you asked him?'

Maryam was reluctant to admit how much she'd been thinking about it. 'No, I haven't said anything to anyone yet. Well,' she amended, 'I just asked Ashikin what she thought and she has a friend ...'

'Who?'

'Rosnah, a friend from school. From Kedai Buloh. She seems like a nice girl.'

'You've met her?'

'You know ... she's met Ashikin for lunch at the market.' She looked embarrassed. 'So naturally, I met her. A sweet girl, I thought.'

'Does Malek know her?' Maryam's brother Malek lived in Kedai Buloh.

Her reluctance faded. 'Yes! He thought they were a good

family. They have rice land, and they buy fish and process it. Canning and stuff. She works for her parents.'

Rubiah nodded. 'You'll have all the *budu* you want.'

'True,' Maryam agreed. 'Malek's going to find out whether there's been any talk of marriage for her. Then maybe we'll see ...' She trailed off, not wanting to sound too enthusiastic yet, lest they find out the girl was already spoken for.

Maryam cleared her throat. 'Who shall we see tomorrow? Zaiton or Murad?'

Rubiah answered immediately. 'Murad. Let Aliza find out some more about Zaiton first. Besides, I'm curious to meet this fair but cheap one. He sounds awful.'

'He probably is.'

Chapter VIII

They took a three-wheeled taxi to Semut Api, anxious to not arrive looking hot and possibly dishevelled; it would never do with someone described as this forbidding. His house was quiet, and Murad himself was ensconced in a chair on the porch.

He was not a large man. He was dark, with pure white hair and beard; his large, beaked nose dominated his narrow face, and his dark eyes were large and hooded. Maryam thought he looked like a hawk – cold and alert, and well capable of violence. He was dressed simply in a cotton sarong and white shirt, with a knitted white cap. He glared down at them from the porch as they approached.

'Hello, *Abang*,' Maryam greeted him, smiling. She refused to show any of the intimidation she felt upon seeing him. He looked at her silently, without moving.

'I am Maryam, and this is Rubiah,' she swept her arm toward her cousin. 'We're here helping the police about this, this ... tragedy. I worked with Jamillah, you know, in the market. We all mourn her.'

He made no indication he had heard her, or even noticed her

standing at the foot of the stairs. 'You are *Abang* Murad, aren't you?' she continued, growing exasperated.

He stood up abruptly. 'What are you doing here, *Kak*? Why have you come to my house?'

She stood her ground. 'I'm here to help the police investigate *Kak* Jamillah's death.'

'And why are you asking?'

'We're helping the police. It's a complicated problem, you see, and we have ...'

'Why are you helping the police?' he continued stubbornly. 'You aren't policemen. I don't see what you have to do with it.' He looked down at them from the porch.

'There is too much of this,' he continued, 'too much of people doing what they want instead of what they should. It's led us here.'

'*Abang*,' Maryam replied, forcing herself to stay reasonable, 'you may be right. Yet, we are here already, and these injustices must be made right.'

She liked the sound of that: important, even altruistic. 'I ask you help us, to find who killed her.'

Murad was silent for a moment, then motioned for them to ascend to the porch. He sat stiffly, offering nothing to eat or drink. His wife peeped out of the door, but he waved her away before she could offer them anything, or even greet them.

'Now,' Maryam began, but Murad held up a warning finger.

'Wait!' he commanded. 'I'll tell you what happened.' He looked down his hawk's nose at them, and narrowed his eyes.

'It's people wanting to get things for nothing that began this.

You think it's alright,' he accused Maryam, though she'd said nothing, and indeed, had not changed expression.

'Well, life doesn't work that way. You have to work for what you get, and work hard. People don't appreciate that, they don't think about it, but they should. They want money handed to them, so they're ready to steal, and, yes, even kill to get what they want. One person like that can poison and corrupt all the other people around. I know it seems harsh. But it's true.'

Maryam, at first confused, decided it was Aziz he was attacking here.

'I think,' he continued, leaning closer to the women, 'someone like that killed Jamillah. That's the kind of person you should look for. Not here.'

'Yes, exactly!' Maryam enthusiastically agreed. 'And that's why we're here, to ask you about *Abang* Aziz. You know him, and perhaps you can tell us – '

Murad looked witheringly at her, then stood up. 'He's just what I was talking about. Money for nothing. Lazy, complaining. I heard him after I sold my boat; he accused me of cheating him.' He looked contemptuous. 'I don't cheat people. I'm fair.'

Maryam thought that if you were fair, it was hardly necessary to proclaim it. After all, if you had to point it out to people, how fair were you?

'I've known him for a long time. We grew up together. He was always like that.'

Rubiah asked bluntly, 'Were you thinking of your son marrying his daughter? I heard it was being discussed.'

He was surprised. 'Where did you hear that? It won't happen.'

Rubiah probed. 'Did you want it to happen?'

'I won't discuss personal things here. My son needs a good strong wife, and we will find one. Aziz's family is not for us.'

How had this become common talk? he wondered. This was Hamidah's doing – his wife and her plans. He knew Aziz would never agree to a wedding between their children, and he wasn't sure he was all that pleased with it himself. He wanted another kind of bride for his son, perhaps the daughter of his sister, Noriah. She would be well brought up, he could be sure of that, but Aziz? Who knew how his daughter would be? Hamidah claimed it would heal the rift between their families, but Murad didn't care if that rift remained. Had she been gossiping?

Maryam looked longingly towards the door of the house. What might she find out from the wife? If only she would come out. But, as she suspected, Murad's wife was too well trained to show her face now, poor soul. Imagine being married to someone like him!

'Don't concern yourself with marriages,' he ordered them. 'You let the police do their job. They won't have to look too long.'

With that, the two visitors were brusquely dismissed. He turned on his heel and went into his house, leaving Maryam and Rubiah staring after him.

Murad walked purposefully to the back of the house, staring down the steps to the kitchen. He hated chattering women prying into his life. He preferred a simple life, uncluttered by people underfoot. Murad could not say he enjoyed the company of women; he was contemptuous of them, and never more so than when watching them work. He avoided the market, where they dominated; just watching them talk and laugh and tease each other and their customers threatened to make him physically ill.

Like these two market women with pretensions of helping the police. He had a good mind to go to Kota Bharu and tell the police chief just what they were up to; no doubt he'd be shocked. Yes, and furious too. He'd like to be there in the room when they were called off their charade of detecting. Perhaps tomorrow ...

In this, he was very different from his wife Hamidah, who enjoyed the company of others. She privately thought he carried a damp fog about him, sucking the fun out of life with his unblinking stares and the way he tightened his lips in disapproval.

Many Kelantanese women, faced with such a bleak husband, would have left long ago and found someone more congenial, both to themselves and their children. But Hamidah and her parents had considered Murad an advantageous match: his family had a good deal of Arab blood (quite prestigious), and he certainly took his responsibility to make a living far more seriously than just about any other man in Kelantan.

Then too, given his fierce condemnation of drinking and gambling, she believed it unlikely he would indulge in the third leg of common vice – women – and that made a nice change from the worries of many of her other friends. And even if Murad wasn't much fun, and forced the family to tiptoe around him for fear of igniting his righteous wrath ... well, he had been away most of the time.

That was then. It was difficult now for her to escape from her dour husband, especially since he had sold his boat and was at home more often. Hamidah had started considering escape. But she'd have to do it carefully, *seperti lotong meniti dahan kayu*: like a monkey making its way across a bough. And like that monkey, one wrong move could find her tumbling to her death.

Chapter IX

'OK, so …' Aliza began, filling her mother in on the teenage news of Kampong Penambang. It was a whole other world.

'His name is Rahim, and he's a fisherman. And his parents have already been to see Zaiton's parents. Her father is considering it, and said he likes him and he works hard.' Maryam thought the same.

'*But,*' she paused for effect, 'her mother didn't like him, and thought Zaiton should marry someone with more money.'

Maryam said mildly that Jamillah may have only wanted what she thought was best for her daughter.

'And Rahim was there for the ceremony, but he left before it ended. He had to get to work the next day and go all the way back to Semut Api.'

Aliza then wrapped up: 'Zaiton says she thinks she'll marry Rahim when things get back to normal. She thinks her father will accept it.'

'Well! That was great. I'm so proud of you. And grateful for your help.'

Aliza glowed. 'I can help some more,' she said with enthusiasm.

'Not now,' Maryam said, a bit more sternly than she'd meant to. 'Don't get involved in this on your own, Aliza. It can turn dangerous.'

* * *

Aziz stood uncertainly in the middle of the yard, surrounded by honking, snapping geese. Mamat had got them during Maryam's last case, when he felt the need to ensure no one came close to the house without being announced. The geese were perfect: they honked loudly, they hissed and they snapped, especially at people they didn't know, although they were capable of making anyone's life miserable, stranger or friend. Aziz had his own geese, and was no neophyte when it came to avoiding being bitten. He protected himself without riling the birds and waited where he was until rescue arrived.

Mamat clattered down the steps, waving the geese away and greeting Aziz. 'It's so nice to see you. Please, come up. Yam! We have a visitor,' he cried, and Maryam soon appeared at the door.

'*Abang* Aziz! How nice to see you. Are you alright? One moment, I just have to get something.' She disappeared into the kitchen and the welcome sounds of rattling dishes signified that coffee was on its way. Aziz seemed pleasantly impatient to receive coffee and snacks, and Mamat wondered whether he'd been eating regularly with Jamillah gone.

'Have you spoken to him?' he demanded of Maryam while she still poured coffee.

'Do you mean Murad?' He nodded, and picked a cake to

accompany his coffee. Mamat leaned forward proffering his box of cigarettes, which Aziz accepted gratefully. Thus prepared, the conversation could continue.

'We saw him,' Maryam said carefully. 'I don't know that it was ... "conclusive" in any way.'

'He hates me.'

'He doesn't seem to like anyone very much.'

'Yes, but me especially. You can see how he would have hurt Jamillah. *Punggong dipukul gigi habis tanggal:* kick the rear end and the teeth fall out. He'd hurt Jamillah to get at me.'

Maryam sat down and lit a cigarette taken from Mamat's box. 'What's this I hear about a wedding for Zaiton?'

Aziz stiffened. 'I'm not even thinking of that right now.'

'But there's been someone interested?'

'A boy from Semut Api,' Aziz told her grudgingly.

'Do you like him?'

Aziz took an exasperated breath. 'Why are we talking about this?'

'It could have some bearing. What about Murad's son?'

Aziz's face and neck became bright red. 'I don't know what you've heard,' he said between clenched teeth, 'but that is completely wrong. I would never agree to have my daughter marry into that family. Never!'

'Does this other boy have hopes?'

Aziz ran his hand over his face. 'You know,' he sighed, 'I haven't been thinking about it much. But why not? He's a nice boy, a hard worker, a nice family. And Zaiton likes him. A lot of parents don't want to take that into account, but I want her to be happy.' He looked hard at Maryam.

'You're absolutely right!' she said warmly. 'I'm so glad to hear you say that!' She beamed at him. He'd just risen infinitely in her estimation. She would never have imagined him saying something so thoughtful, and at that moment she decided she really didn't want it to be Aziz who killed Jamillah. There would have to be someone else.

'So,' she began, leaning forward towards him, 'who do you think wanted Murad's son to marry her? Not you or Jamillah, right?'

He shrugged. 'Me, definitely not. Jamillah, bless her, I don't think so. To be frank, she wanted someone with some money for Zaiton, or at least more money than this boy Rahim has, but saying that doesn't necessarily mean she wanted Kamal. Murad? Never. So, that would leave Hamidah, his wife. I never hear her talk anymore, so I don't know.'

'Anymore?'

'We grew up together, you know; all of us, in Semut Api. She was very spirited; laughed a lot, flirted. I mean, this was a long time ago! *Seperti gading dilarek:* like polished ivory she was, a pretty girl.

'Murad was quite a catch in the *kampong*. They had money and he would captain his own boat. Mind you, the family was never a friendly one. Murad is just like his father: never happy, never talking. No fun at all. Well, *harimau menunjokkan belangnya:* the tiger shows his stripes, you know. You can't avoid blood.'

He took a sip of coffee and, with that, the flow of homilies paused. It was a good thing, too, or Maryam's new-found respect for Aziz might well have dissolved.

'I was surprised when she married him. I mean, I know most parents want their daughters to be comfortable; I want it for my own girls. But they knew the family and how miserable they were! And let me tell you ...'

Maryam braced herself for another nugget of wisdom. 'After a few months of being married to him, you never saw her anymore. She was a like a ghost. If she was out, she was silent, her head down, never talking to anyone. Like the life had been sucked out of her. Now,' he turned to Mamat, 'why would I ever let my girl marry into a family like that?'

Mamat nodded. 'Never!' he averred.

'But you invested in his boat,' Maryam mused.

He snorted. 'Business is business, *Kakak*! That's not marrying him!'

She had to agree.

* * *

Osman made his familiar way down the aisles of the main market towards Maryam's stall. Why was he always finding her to ask what happened, and never Maryam volunteering information to him? He pondered that unhappily.

But it was only another few days before he left for Perak to be married, a thought which cheered him up immeasurably. Now he would pass from the not particularly gentle ministrations of Maryam and Rubiah to the more familiar orders of his own mother. He wouldn't need to make a single decision about anything while he was home!

He was unsure of what his married life would be. He vaguely remembered this cousin who would be his bride, but he never knew her. However, his mother's side of the family definitely ran to strong women, so it was entirely possible that, young and sweet-looking as she was, she had a core of steel on which he could lean. He couldn't accurately say whether this pleased him or terrified him.

'Ah, it's you!' Maryam greeted him from her perch atop her counter. Her immediate neighbour, Rashidah, peered around the divider and smiled. 'Come to get your *kain songket* for the wedding now?'

Osman tried to staunch the current carrying him away from his chosen conversation. 'Well, I don't ...'

'Of course, he is!' Rashidah hopped off her own counter to stand in front of Maryam's. 'You must be leaving for Perak very soon.'

'Yes, I ...'

'Cream!' Maryam announced, overriding his half-hearted mumbling. 'I said so before, right, Dah? It's all the colour right now.'

Rashidah agreed enthusiastically and helped Maryam open an especially heavy piece of creamy silk, shot through with gold threads that appeared and disappeared in the fabric. Maryam was triumphant. 'It's a beauty, isn't it?' Rashidah stroked it appreciatively. 'Gorgeous.' They both looked expectantly at Osman.

'Well, I think ...'

'I told you,' Maryam said to Rashidah, smiling broadly. 'I knew he'd like it. And his wife ... well, she's bound to love it.'

'Of course,' she agreed. 'Is the rest of the wedding in cream as well?'

'I don't really ...'

'Yes, why would the groom be involved in that?' Maryam asked rhetorically. 'I mean, he's here, working.' She turned to Osman as she expertly folded yards of fabric into a rather large bundle. 'You just tell her,' she advised him, 'that you've got wonderful *songket*.'

'Made right here!' Rashidah interjected.

'Where else? And that it's cream! She'll know what else to do, believe me.' She and Rashidah laughed merrily. They'd seen this before.

'But I wanted ...'

'What?' asked Maryam kindly, handing him a skilfully wrapped package which weighed a lot more than it appeared it would.

'To talk to you,' he finished lamely. 'About the case.'

'Ah.' Maryam regarded him expressionlessly. 'Go ahead.'

Now he felt lost. 'Well, *Mak Cik* ... I mean, what's happened?'

Maryam sighed and shook her head. 'Go up to Rubiah then and ask her to come, and we'll tell you together. And bring some coffee and *onde-onde*.' She watched him leave, and as he passed Rashidah, he knew she watched him too and thought him an ungrateful whelp for bringing this into the presentation of such a fine piece of *songket*. He felt guilty, but reminded himself, as he trudged up the stairs, that he was the chief of police!

* * *

Maryam and Rubiah slowly descended from their trishaw, shielding their eyes from the sun. Though it was low in the sky already, throwing long and slanting shadows, it was still damnably hot. On the sand at Pantai Cinta Berahi, brilliantly painted fishing boats were pulled up along the shore, the crews carefully stowing their equipment while fish wholesalers were wrapping up their stock amid large chunks of ice in stout wooden boxes. They searched anxiously for Rahim.

'Do you think he's already left?' Rubiah asked worriedly. 'Maybe we should have reached here right when the boats came in …'

Maryam shook her head. 'And be so conspicuous? How would that look for Rahim?' She narrowed her eyes and tried to pick him out of a crowd of sunburned young men with batik kerchiefs tied around their heads. It was tough going.

After their first circumambulation of the boats, one man detached himself from the crowd and presented himself to them – a blessing, for otherwise Maryam was convinced they would never find him, and she wasn't sure she cared to continue walking on the sand. However, here he was.

'*Mak Cik*? What are you doing here?'

'Rahim!' Relief flooded her voice. 'I'm so glad to see you,' she told him fervently.

He was surprised by her intensity. 'Why? What's wrong?'

She felt she may have been too emotional in her greeting. 'Nothing, really. But it's so hot!'

Rahim grinned at her. 'No trees.'

'I see, yes.' Maryam sought to compose herself. 'Well, it's only that I had a few questions, no more than that.'

'Well, something to drink first!' He led them off the sand to a wooden bench under a coconut palm. 'Wait here.'

'Such a nice boy,' Rubiah sighed as he walked off to find some cold drinks. 'Aziz should be pleased to have such a son-in-law.'

Maryam nodded; it was true. Lovely manners, even after a full day's hard work, which said a great deal for his character. 'I don't see how he could be involved in a murder himself,' Rubiah stated firmly. 'He's not that kind of man.'

Maryam raised an eyebrow, and fanned herself with the ends of her headcloth. 'Anyone could be that kind of man.'

As Rahim returned, carrying three bags of iced tea, she reflected that she didn't really think he was that kind of man, either. But to admit it meant she wasn't really looking for the real killer, she would only be looking for someone she didn't like who might plausibly kill. This was a completely different kind of search, and not one she cared to find herself undertaking. She sighed. It was hard meeting people you liked in the course of an investigation.

'What did you want to ask me?' Rahim took a long pull on his straw.

'You know *Pak Cik* Murad pretty well, don't you?'

He shrugged.

'You've worked for him. You must know him, perhaps better than you think.'

'Listen, *Mak Cik*,' he began hesitantly, 'I don't really know what to say. You see, he's a rich man around here. He's made a lot of money. Is he a better captain than all the others?' He paused. 'No. He's good, I mean, he knows what he's doing, but no captain lasts long if he doesn't.

'He's tight-fisted,' he stated flatly. 'He hardly spends anything. He won't even treat his crew to drinks!' He shook his head. 'I don't know if you can get rich that way, but he's certainly tried.'

Rahim wiped his sunburned face again, and waved another one of his crew over to them. 'Mat,' he said simply. Mat nodded and sat on the ground with his back to the trunk of the palm. 'She wants to know about Murad,' he explained. 'How he got rich and what kind of a captain he was.'

'The kind who never spent a cent,' Mat stated firmly. He lowered his voice and looked hard at Rahim. 'But they say ...'

The two men carried on a silent conversation as Maryam watched them. It seemed as though they came to a conclusion, and Mat cleared his throat.

'That is, they say, you know ...' he hesitated, and Maryam forbore to encourage him, fearing he would stop altogether. 'His family has had, well, a pelesit, they say. For a long time.' He nodded again, and looked around furtively, as though the very mention of a familiar spirit might summon it to appear before him.

'Really?' Rubiah asked. 'And that's how he got rich, through this evil spirit?'

Rahim answered, his eyes still on Mat. 'He keeps it in a bottle,' he added, his voice hardly above a whisper. 'I've seen it on board sometimes. It looks like a grasshopper.'

'He feeds it on his blood,' Mat murmured. 'You know, he pricks his finger to feed it. Or his wife does, and it's robbed her of her mind. And it goes out and brings back money for him. Or makes sure money comes to him,' he amended.

Rahim picked up the thread. 'It's not just fishing. How do you think they got all the rice land they have?' Maryam looked interested, but said nothing.

'They got it all during the war, the Japanese time. People were losing their land left, right and centre, families had nothing to eat except what they could catch. But this family collected land. They never suffered when the Japanese were here.'

Maryam had heard of families collaborating with the Japanese and growing wealthy, but didn't expect to run into one of them here, now.

'But,' she sputtered, 'do they still have it?'

The two men nodded solemnly. 'They never let go of anything they get,' Rahim assured her. 'They still have it.'

'It isn't just the Japanese, it's that evil spirit as well. And you don't want to talk about it too much, in case Murad notices. He could send it after you, *Mak Cik*, to punish you for talking about it.' He was speaking faster now, more nervously. 'Maybe I shouldn't say anything, but you must be careful.'

'He still has it,' Mat added. 'It's still active. Believe me. The other owner of his boat didn't make much when he sold it. Just him.'

Mat then stood up to leave and said his goodbyes. Rahim stood to follow him, but first dug his toe into the sand and kept his gaze on it.

'You must be careful,' he said softly. 'You don't know how he could be if he thought you were after him. And his pelesit, it knows things, and it won't like you asking questions. You may not believe me,' he lifted his head suddenly, and looked right at her, 'but I'm telling you the truth.'

He looked around nervously, then leaned forward to them. 'Look what happened to *Mak Cik* Jamillah!'

'Was that the pelesit? Why?'

Rahim appeared to be in an agony of apprehension. He whispered again. 'It didn't want her asking questions about the boat! It's protecting the money!

'They say,' he added hoarsely, 'there was a huge grasshopper in her yard for the next couple of days, and no one could kill it.'

With an anguished glance, he said goodbye and began to walk away. But his manners got the better of him.

'Come,' he said, returning to them. 'I'll find you a taxi.'

Chapter X

It happened so fast, Maryam could never really remember the order of events. She had just left her yard with a particularly good batch of *nasi kerabu* which she felt she must share with Rubiah (who ought to have been impressed, it was really that good) when she was felled by a hard smack across her forehead, which dropped her unconscious onto the path before she could utter a sound.

The heavy stick with which she was hit made a solid thud as it connected, and this alarmed the geese. Their frantic honking and flapping brought Mamat down the steps to investigate, and in the dark, it took him a few moments to see Maryam lying still and silent, the plate shattered and *nasi kerabu* flung to the ground.

He did not remember calling out as he rushed to her, but it brought the neighbours, who helped him carry her into the house and lay her down on the couch. In the light, he could see her forehead, already swelling around a braided mark. They all recognized it: the *enam sembilan*, or 6-9, was a traditional Kelantanese weapon, generally used to teach a lesson rather than for mayhem. A club wrapped in thick rope at both ends, it could pack a wallop, and also left a distinctive bruise – the rope pattern. It was not used to kill, but to humiliate.

Aliza slipped out of the door, walking around the edges of the small crowd surrounding her mother. She stood on tiptoe, peering over the shoulders of the neighbours to see her mother lying deathly still on their living room couch and her father's panicked face. She also heard the murmuring of concerned neighbours. She went silently and swiftly through the *kampong* to Rubiah's house, arriving out of breath and with growing anxiety.

'*Mak Su*!'

Rubiah came to the door, wiping her hands with a dishrag. 'Liza? What's happened?' She took in Aliza's red face and the tears starting to stream.

'My mother, *Mak Su*! Someone hit her on the head! It looks like she might be … dying!'

'*Astaghfirullah*!' Rubiah cried, 'I'm on my way.' She hurried down the stairs, followed by a frightened Aliza. As they hurried past Aziz's house, Zaiton called to her from the top of the stairs.

'Liza! Where are you going?'

'Something's happened to my mother,' Aliza told her, calling from over her shoulder as she ran home.

'What?'

'I think she was hit with something. Over the head.'

'No!' Zaiton ran down the stairs and clasped Aliza's hand, pulling her towards the house. 'Tell me what happened!' she demanded.

Aliza pulled her hand away. 'I don't know yet, I have to go back home!'

'Wait!' Zaiton tugged at her harder, pulling her off her feet.

'What are you doing?' Aliza was becoming frightened, this girl no longer seemed like the one she knew.

'Aliza?'

'What?'

'Come with me.'

'Let me get up,' she said slowly. 'Wait a minute.' She got up gingerly, feeling her knees, testing them, to see if they had been hurt. It appeared they had not. She limped a few steps toward Zaiton. 'What do you want?'

'Nothing.' The two girls stared at each other. 'Just come with me to my house.'

Aliza shook her head. 'Why?'

'Just so we can talk.' Zaiton tried to smile and take Aliza's hand again. Before she could grasp it, Aliza whirled away and ran as fast as she could towards her own house.

'*Ayah*!' she screamed as she ran, '*Ayah*! Help me!' She tripped on a large rock, and was flung headfirst onto the path, hitting her head as she fell.

As she passed, neighbours poked their heads out the windows and started down off their porches. Aliza lay dazed in the dust, her head seeming to pour blood on the ground. Zaiton, in hot pursuit, almost fell on top of her, but was seized in the unyielding grasp of one of their neighbours.

Three women pulled Aliza to her feet and started walking her home; she was barely conscious. They half-walked, half-dragged her into her own yard, where her sister Ashikin was already running towards her. When she reached Aliza, she folded her into her arms.

'*Adik*!' Aliza pitched forward in a dead faint, bringing both of them to the ground.

Daud, Ashikin's husband, was there immediately, standing in front of them both to protect them, while Ashikin called for help. Zaiton was soon frog-marched in, held in the unsympathetic grasp of two of their burlier neighbours.

'What's this?' Daud demanded of Zaiton.

She stared up at him, her eyes wide, unable to speak. Aziz now burst into the yard, stopping short before he tripped over his daughter. He looked wildly from Daud to Zaiton, taking in Ashikin and Aliza sheltered behind him. 'Why?' he finally asked Zaiton. She burst into tears.

'We saw Aliza fall,' one of the burly men said sternly. 'Zaiton was chasing her, and she tripped on a rock.' He then turned to Daud and spoke kindly to him.

'These head wounds bleed a lot,' he explained, 'but she still needs a doctor.'

Daud and the neighbours were now in animated discussion with Aziz while Zaiton crouched behind her father, wailing. The men ignored her, while the women went inside for cloth and water.

'I don't know what she's doing or why,' Aziz insisted heatedly to Daud. 'I only heard someone fall, so I went out to look.'

Daud turned his most threatening face to Zaiton. Had she not been beside herself, she would probably have remained serenely unthreatened. But she was now caught up in her own hysteria and beginning to choke on her sobs. 'Where's Rahim?' she babbled. 'Is he inside?'

'Rahim?' Aziz looked momentarily mystified, and then horrified. 'Is he here? Did you see him tonight?'

Zaiton continued crying, and in towering frustration, her father slapped her, hard. She fell silent immediately. He looked over at Daud, abashed, but relieved to have quieted her. 'Now, tell me!' He commanded her. 'Where is he?'

'I don't know!' She threatened to break into tears again, but a good look at her father's face convinced her to avoid it. 'I thought maybe ...'

Osman shouldered his way into the crowd, and looked down with evident surprise at the girl squatting in the dirt.

'She tried to grab Aliza,' Daud explained quickly. 'She chased her to stop her from coming home, and she tripped on a rock. We need a doctor here too.'

Osman turned and signalled his men; the doctor was now working on Maryam and would next move on to Aliza. Osman hated to see the whole family involved.

'We're trying to find out why. Which is hard!' Daud added in frustration.

Osman turned to Zaiton, 'Well?'

'I was looking for Rahim.'

Osman looked confused. 'Why Rahim? Why Aliza?'

Zaiton gave a monumental sniff and looked around the faces before her. None seemed particularly sympathetic – or that patient, for that matter. She decided it best to talk quickly, before her father moved to hurry things along again.

'I thought he might be here. Because, you see ...'

Aziz snorted impatiently. 'Listen to me, daughter, you'd better talk and talk fast, or else ...'

'I thought he might come here to talk to *Mak Cik* Maryam. About my mother's death. If he were here, I wanted ... to know,' she finished lamely.

'Did you think he might hurt her?'

'No! Of course not! No, I just wanted to find out what happened to *Mak Cik* Maryam.' She turned to her father and spoke rapidly. 'He wouldn't hurt anyone, *Ayah*. He's a good man. No, I wasn't worried about that, just that I didn't know what happened, so I was ... worried.'

'What did she say?' Osman asked Daud, cursing himself again for not understanding.

'She only wanted to find out what happened.'

The doctor came down the stairs, looking for his next patient. 'How is my mother?' Ashikin asked while cradling the still quiet Aliza.

He grunted. 'I'm putting her in the hospital now; it's just to be on the safe side. Concussion possibly. But we have to be careful. That's going to leave a nasty bruise, I haven't seen an *enam sembilan* attack for ... I don't know how long. What's it about?'

Ashikin shrugged.

'Another concussion? What's going on here?' The doctor then knelt down next to Aliza, looking concerned. He wiped away the blood, still streaming down her forehead. He shook his head sadly.

'She's also going to the hospital. Her daughter?' Ashikin nodded, tears spilling from her large eyes.

'They should go quickly,' he said to Osman. 'I'll go with them.'

Moments later, an ambulance came screaming into the *kampong*, lights flashing. Maryam, Aliza and the doctor, accompanied by several policemen with strict orders not to let the two women out of their sight, were soon rushing back to Kota Bharu.

Chapter XI

Osman thought he would go mad with worry. He had patrolled the hallways of the Kota Bharu General Hospital too often. In fact, Rahman (his sidekick, as he thought of him) had only recently been released after a serious head injury nearly cashiered him. And now Maryam and – worse – her young daughter were here with similar injuries. (Although, he fervently prayed, not as critical as Rahman's.) He ought never to have asked Maryam to help him, but how was he to know her daughter would also get involved? He peeked into their rooms, and continued to pace the corridors.

Maryam was awake, but groggy, constantly running her fingers along the heavy rope pattern on her forehead. Mixed into her anger and fear was humiliation: she had been branded a busybody, carrying a mark every Kelantanese would recognize as a warning to cease interfering. Never mind that she was working at the express request– no, *demand* – of the police. That might not be immediately apparent, but the mark she now bore certainly was.

She had not yet been told about Aliza, and Mamat was dreading the conversation. He wasn't sure why he was feeling so guilty; he had never encouraged Aliza to be involved, and had not known she was. (Even if she was, he didn't feel he had a real grasp of the story). But he felt obscurely that, as her father, he should have somehow known and stopped it. He thought grimly he should put a stop to it now, and also insist that Maryam stop investigating, once and for all, but he also knew that now she would never give it up until she found out who had done such a thing – not only to her, but to her daughter as well. He sat outside Aliza's room, his head in his hands, considering his inability to protect his family, and occasionally, when he heard Osman's footsteps, lifting his head to glare at him.

Aliza had narrowly avoided serious damage, but had a large and ugly scar on the back of her head which had, of necessity, been shaved. It wrung Mamat's heart to see her without her hair, looking so small and vulnerable. Ashikin spent most of the days she had been in the hospital sitting with her, even sleeping there with her.

Ashikin had also called her brother Azmi, serving in the army, who had been granted leave and rushed back to Kota Bharu. Maryam had been amazed and delighted to see him, but it frightened her too. She had begun to suspect, in a confused sort of way, that something else was terribly wrong. Why else would Azmi have left camp to come back?

The family gathered in Maryam's room, and she watched with mounting fear as they all walked solemnly in, even Yi carrying Ashikin's daughter Nuraini. At any other time, this would have set off a torrent of baby talk and delighted smiles all around, but now only Yi paid attention to her. 'Where's Aliza?' Maryam asked, not as clearly as she would have liked.

Mamat looked uncomfortable, and took her hands. Maryam began to cry. 'What's happened to her? Is she dead?'

'Why would you think that?' Mamat cried. He flinched from the very thought.

'No, *Mak*,' Ashikin swiftly took over. 'She'll be fine. She's here too. I've been with her the whole time.'

'Tell me.' Maryam attempted to stop crying, but could not. Mamat sat next to her, his arm around her shoulder, trying to calm her. '*Sayang*, she ran to get Rubiah when you were hurt. And on the way back, you see, Zaiton tried to grab her, and …'

'Why?'

'It seems Zaiton thought Rahim … is that the right name?' Ashikin nodded. 'She thought Rahim was there, when you were hurt. That she thought Rahim had hurt you.'

'Rahim?' Maryam seemed dizzy.

'Well, that's what she said. And she grabbed Aliza when she was coming back home, and Aliza fought with her to get free, and she fell.' Mamat sat silent.

'And …' Maryam prompted.

'And she hit her head on a rock.'

Maryam began crying again. 'Oh no! It can't be!' She looked around. 'Where is she? Is she alright?'

'She's getting better,' Ashikin assured her. 'She still doesn't remember what happened very well, but the doctor says she'll be fine.'

'They had to shave her head!' Yi piped up.

Maryam stared at him. 'Oh no! When can I see her? I want to see her right now!' She climbed out of the bed and stood up, looked around, and fainted. Mamat caught her and placed her back on the bed, with Azmi's help. 'You didn't have to tell her that!' Azmi told Yi. 'She didn't need to know that right away!'

'Stop,' Mamat said tiredly. 'She'd find out anyway. It doesn't matter.' He turned to Ashikin. 'Can she walk yet?'

She shook her head. 'Not yet, but Aliza's young. She'll be better very soon.'

'I can't take both of them sick.' Mamat sat down suddenly on the bed. 'I just can't.' Ashikin sat next to him with her arms around him.

'We can help, *Ayah*.' She gave Azmi a meaningful look.

'I'm here now,' Azmi said, taking his cue. Azmi was tall and lean, and looked a great deal like his father, with high cheekbones and large eyes. The army had whipped him into excellent shape, and he was strong and confident, a son both Maryam and Mamat were immensely proud of, and certainly, in this dire situation, a welcome source from which the whole family could draw strength.

His father, for the first time that Azmi could remember, looked haggard, and his strong-willed mother had just passed out. He felt as though he had entered an alternate universe, where the parents who had always cared for him, sometimes more than he wanted, now looked to him for guidance. He and Ashikin would have to care for their family.

He'd seen Aliza, so fragile with her head shaved, looking like an injured bird, and Yi, lost with no one to care for him. Daud was taking him home to his own family, ostensibly to help with Nuraini's care, but mostly to have him safe and surrounded by family. It was clear Ashikin was needed by her parents, and he could at least take Yi off her mind.

Osman stuck his head in the room, frowning at the tableau confronting him. Azmi and Ashikin led him into the hallway and sat him down.

'You can see,' Azmi began, stern in his uniform, 'my parents are exhausted. My mother has to rest, and I'm afraid my father is worried to death. Look what's happened here! My little sister is hurt, my mother is hurt ... don't you think this is too dangerous for them?' Azmi demanded.

Ashikin frowned at Osman, and he actually felt a little frightened. 'I had no idea your sister would have done anything ...'

Ashikin cut him off mercilessly. 'We're all involved now. Tell us, have you found Rahim?'

'I'm not sure I really should talk about it.'

'Surely, you can try,' Azmi wheedled politely. 'I mean, we are all in it now.'

'I understand,' Osman replied, equally polite, 'but perhaps ...'

'You understand?' Ashikin hissed at him. 'After what's happened to my mother and sister, you're not sure? *Cik* Osman, I can't accept that.' She paused, giving him a moment to contemplate his failings.

'Now,' she ordered him, 'tell me what you've found.' She put her hands on her hips and narrowed her beautiful eyes.

Azmi shrugged his shoulders minimally, and Osman understood he could expect no help there. He sighed. And began speaking.

'We can't find Rahim. We've gone to Semut Api, and no one's seen him since the evening your mother was hurt. No one knows where he is, or ...' he amended, 'no one's saying.

'Zaiton doesn't have a very coherent story to tell, though I think if I leave her father to it, it will get clearer. She was afraid Rahim was at your mother's, which I interpret to mean she was afraid Rahim had attacked your mother. And as best as I can understand – and I'm no expert on female psychology – ' Ashikin rolled her eyes and he quailed, 'she had some vague plan about grabbing Aliza and holding her as a kind of hostage in case Rahim was involved.'

'That's ridiculous!'

'I know, but I do think that was her plan ... If you can say she actually had one. It seems she acted more on impulse.'

'Why would Rahim attack my mother? I thought she liked him.'

Now Osman shrugged. 'If he did, which we don't know, maybe he wanted to stop her from investigating.'

Ashikin seemed to relent slightly once he'd begun to talk. He reflected that she would make an excellent interrogator. She was small, but very intimidating.

'Zaiton knows more than she's saying,' she announced, more to her brother than to Osman. 'No one is that confused. She might think she can get away with it talking to a group of men who don't want to make her cry, but I'm sure I can get the truth out of her.'

Osman agreed wholeheartedly. If he were Zaiton, he'd start

talking as soon as Ashikin entered the room. Though it was possible Zaiton herself had more steel in her than he had imagined.

'I can go over with *Mak Su* Rubiah,' she decided. 'Mi, can you watch Aliza?' He nodded. She turned to Osman: 'Can you drive me home?' He also nodded, and did as he was told.

* * *

Ashikin and Rubiah arrived at Aziz's home as they were; there had been no consideration of what to wear or with how much jewellery. Rubiah carried a small packet of cakes which she pressed into Aziz's hands when they arrived, but small talk was kept to a minimum.

'I think you know why we're here, *Abang*,' Rubiah greeted him. 'We must speak with Zaiton.'

He nodded and waved them into the house. 'You'd better answer them, and no fooling around,' he told her sternly, and then retreated to the porch, where he could hear the conversation but did not appear to be part of it. He lit a cigarette, his head cocked towards the door.

'Coffee?' Zaiton asked, trying for a social tone. Ashikin agreed, but hardly unbent. Rubiah took her cigarettes from the fold of her sarong and passed one to Ashikin. She did not offer any to Zaiton, who was not yet married.

'Zaiton,' Ashikin cooed when she'd sat down, 'you know Aliza is in the hospital now. Just avoided being killed! *Alhamdulillah*.' The others echoed her.

'But I'm still not sure what happened. Oh, I heard from

the police,' she waved her arm as though scattering useless information, 'but let's be frank, they didn't really know what you were talking about. And maybe they were too polite to push you too hard, you know, as you were crying.' Here both Rubiah and Ashikin tightened their lips and looked hard at her.

'But we're all women here, we know truth from lies, right?' Zaiton looked from one to the other. 'And I'd like some answers,' Ashikin finished, taking a small sip from her coffee and tapping her cigarette on the saucer. They waited in silence for Zaiton to respond.

At her first sniff, Ashikin immediately rebuked her. 'No crying now. We aren't impressed by it, and I've got to get back to the hospital to watch Aliza. You can cry later if you want, but not on my time. Come on!'

Zaiton twisted her hands for a few moments, but as soon as Ashikin reached for the younger woman, no doubt to administer a sharp slap to still her, she stopped. 'Oh, I don't know what to say!'

'Tell the truth!' Ashikin ordered her in her flintiest voice.

She sighed. 'You know I'm going to marry Rahim. Well, that is to say, it isn't completely set, but I think it's definitely happening. He's a good man, and he works hard.'

'And?'

'And, well, *Pak Cik* Murad's been horrible to him!' she burst out. 'He's horrible to everyone! He has a pelesit,' she lowered her voice, 'and it does whatever he tells it. It drinks his blood. Rahim's seen it.'

'So?'

'So? He's a frightening and evil man! You know what a spirit like that can do. It takes money from everyone else and brings it to him! That's why he has so much and other people all lose when they invest with him! My father did, and look what happened! And he would even take it on his boat, and that's where Rahim saw it. It brought the fish to his nets and left other boats with no catch at all.'

'What has this got to do with my mother?'

'This *Pak Cik* Murad, he spoke to Rahim the other day, and he told him that he'd be found guilty of killing my mother, which he didn't do, wouldn't ever do. Rahim knows *Pak Cik* Murad is setting the spirit to catch him, to have him be accused while Murad walks free.'

'Then *Pak Cik* Murad killed your mother?'

'Or the pelesit!' she whispered.

'Can we leave the pelesit out of this for now? There are enough people running around who could have done it without inviting in *jinn*.'

'But don't you see? My mother was killed when we were all here, my father sleeping next to her. How could a person, a full-grown person, have come in without waking anyone, kill her without a sound, and leave? Think about it.'

'And you're telling me this pelesit hit my mother over her head? And where was Rahim?'

'Well, I was afraid he might, might have lost his mind! Yes, the worry, the fear! He would try to stop your mother from going on with this investigation!'

'Zaiton,' Ashikin said angrily. 'You aren't making any sense.

Why did you think Rahim was with my mother?'

'He said he might talk to her. The day before, he said he might have to talk to her to tell her what Murad was going to do. So she would know and not believe him.'

'And you thought he then might have hit her over the head?'

'Maybe she didn't believe him.'

'No one spoke to her before she was hit. She was leaving the house to come and see me,' Rubiah added.

'Are you sure? No one spoke to her on the road?'

'So you're telling me it was Rahim who hit her.'

'No,' she wailed, 'You don't understand.'

'Did you do it?'

'Me?'

'Did you want my mother to stop so you could marry Rahim without worrying about Murad any further? But why grab Aliza?'

Looking exceptionally miserable, Zaiton mumbled, 'If Rahim did do it, I thought maybe I would have Aliza, and then they would let him go.'

'Have Aliza? You mean, kidnap her?'

'I guess.'

Ashikin was amused. 'And keep her where?'

'Here.' She looked around the room.

'And your father wouldn't say a word.'

'Well ...'

'You didn't think this through, did you?'

'Maybe not.'

'No. But you've gotten yourself into a lot of trouble. And where is Rahim now?'

'I don't know.' She hung her head.

'What do you mean?'

'I know he isn't at home, in Semut Api. Maybe he's gone to Thailand?'

'That looks pretty guilty to me.'

'Oh, but he isn't! He didn't want my mother dead!'

'Did he want mine?'

Zaiton gaped at her, for all the world like a hooked mackerel, Ashikin thought. And though she moved her mouth, no words came out: how could they? What more was there to say.

Chapter XII

'*Mak Su* Rubiah, tell me what you think!'

On the porch, the two sat smoking cigarettes. Ashikin felt Aliza's absence keenly; ordinarily she would have been making coffee, listening to the conversation, sitting by the door. And now she was lying in a hospital bed.

'I'm ignoring the whole pelesit thing,' Rubiah said briskly, 'although it's strange someone could get into a full house and kill Jamillah without anyone hearing a thing.'

'Unless it was someone in the house to begin with.'

'Exactly,' Rubiah said approvingly. 'But, back to your mother and Aliza, poor thing. It could be Murad himself, or Rahim, or actually Zaiton.'

'That doesn't help at all.'

'No, but first, let's find Rahim. Thailand?' she said. 'That's a job for Osman. We've got to get back to the hospital.'

* * *

Aziz walked slowly into the main police station on Jalan Ibrahim in Kota Bharu. He had rarely had reason to visit before, and was visibly uncomfortable. Standing stiffly before the front desk, he asked for Osman, and the young desk sergeant importantly asked his business.

'I will tell him myself,' Aziz said slowly. 'I must speak to him directly.'

'I don't know if that's possible,' the officer said airily. 'I've got to make sure first, you know, that he can see you.'

'He knows me. He's investigating my wife's death.'

'A suspect, then!' He rose and walked around the desk, and reached out to take Aziz's arm. Before he could grasp it, Aziz pulled back, and pushed him away, knocking him back against the desk, scattering paperclips all over the floor. The commotion brought other policeman over, roughly grabbing at Aziz as their fallen colleague stumbled and tried to right himself.

'I don't know what you think you're doing,' an older man began, 'but you don't treat policemen like that, and especially not here at the station.'

'I need to see Chief Osman,' Aziz cried loudly as he wrestled several officers. 'I need to see him now!'

Osman came out of his office to find Aziz on the bottom of a scrum. 'What's this?' he asked.

The sergeant stood breathlessly, his uniform somewhat askew, his hair sticking up. 'This man came in to see you, sir, and I realized he was a suspect. He resisted me! So we have disarmed him.'

'Was he armed?'

'Well, no, not really. But he was fighting us.'

Osman shook his head and looked unhappily at all of them. 'He's part of an investigation. Why are you wrestling with him?'

'I just asked to see you.' Aziz was muffled as he was now being helped up and dusted off. 'I didn't expect this!'

'Of course not!' Osman soothed him as he guided him into his office. He jerked his chin at the sergeant, signalling for coffee and cakes. Aziz would need to be mollified.

'I'm so sorry, *Pak Cik*,' Osman began. 'I feel terrible at the way you were treated.'

'Why did they do that?' Aziz asked, 'I just came in here and asked for you.'

'I honestly don't know. Ah! Here's some hot coffee for you … and curry puffs. Please, *Pak Cik* , have something to drink. You'll feel better.'

Osman gave him a big smile, which he turned off as he looked towards the man bringing in the refreshments, who blushed and quickly retreated.

'Tell me now, why did you come here?'

'I can't find Zaiton.'

'What?'

'She's gone, she's left. My older daughter thinks she's gone to Thailand to find Rahim.'

'But why run away?' Osman cursed himself for not taking her into custody. How could he explain losing a suspect?

'Maybe to marry him. Maybe to protect him.' *Or protect herself*, Osman thought, but wouldn't say. 'To get away from Murad, who wants to marry her to his son!'

'Really?'

‘Yes,’ he said shortly. ‘Shouldn’t you be finding my daughter before something happens to her? What if she’s run away to get married in Sungei Golok?’

‘Is that where you think Rahim might have gone?’

‘I heard,’ he said expansively, ‘he had relatives outside Sungei Golok.’

‘Why didn’t you say so earlier?’

‘I didn’t know then. And I don’t know now, but it’s a place to start.’

‘Could your older daughter help us?’

He nodded. ‘Yes, we’d do anything to get her back.’

‘Let me talk to her,’ Osman said, picking up his hat and calling for one of the men to drive. Maybe he could find both of them at once, and get the truth out of them.

Chapter XIII

Maryam had left the hospital and returned home, though she was now wearing a headscarf down low on her forehead to hide the mark of the *enam sembilan*. With Ashikin caring for the family, and Aliza still recovering from her injury, there was no one she trusted to take over the stall, which had remained closed for over a week. That had never happened before, and Maryam was anxious to get things back to normal as quickly as possible.

Aliza was mending and her previously boundless energy now reasserted itself. When she first realized she was now bald, she cried for a day and wouldn't be comforted. 'I'm a freak!' she wailed to Ashikin, 'No one could be this ugly!'

'It's only hair,' Ashikin reminded her. 'It'll grow back.'

In response, Aliza buried her head in the pillow. Azmi walked in on the scene. 'Are you alright?' he asked, alarmed.

'It's just her hair.'

'Just?' came the indignant cry. 'How would you feel ...?'

'I know,' Ashikin sought to control her irritation, remembering what Aliza had just been through. 'Azmi, what do you think?'

'Well, I'm a man, so what do I know? But if you ask me, you

look beautiful even without hair, and as *Kakak* says, it's going to grow back before you know it.'

Aliza did not lift up her head. '*Abang*,' Ashikin began, 'have you ever thought about getting married?'

Azmi stood stock still, and even Aliza was silent. 'Why?'

'I'm just asking.'

'You have someone,' he said flatly, knowing she would never bring this up as idle chatter.

Ashikin shrugged. 'I could suggest someone, if you like.'

'You've already started something,' he stated, not knowing whether he was angry or excited.

'No, just talking to *Mak* about it. You're old enough, you know.'

'That's true,' Aliza chimed in.

'You stay out of this,' he commanded her. 'Who?'

'Well, I'm not sure. But I was thinking maybe of Rosnah. Do you remember her?'

He thought hard. 'I don't think so.'

'She went to school with me.'

'Is she pretty?'

'Of course, she's pretty!'

'Very pretty!' Aliza added, now sitting up on the bed, her hair forgotten. 'She's nice, too.'

Azmi gave her a gentle shove. 'How far has this gone?'

'It hasn't gone anywhere. I'm just asking.'

'Uh huh.'

* * *

Before leaving for southern Thailand, Osman devoted himself to finding out who had attacked Maryam, but the more closely he looked, the larger the body of suspects grew. Aziz said he was home, but no one was there who had seen him. Rahim fled to Thailand, Zaiton was wandering around contemplating mayhem, and her older sister Zainab claimed to have been picking up a few things at a nearby stall, though the timeline was vague.

Murad refused to account for his whereabouts at the time, which Osman took to mean he wasn't anywhere which would definitively clear him, and was therefore possibly the attacker. His wife, whose name Osman could not remember, was almost a wraith, and seemed to have trouble understanding what he was asking her. He wondered whether she was quite sane.

He asked Murad if he could speak to her, and Murad snorted in disgust. 'If you think it will do any good,' he answered, accurately foretelling how Osman would feel after meeting her.

She was timid, and seemed afraid of her husband, who roughly (and, Osman thought, quite rudely) gestured for her to meet him. Murad then illustrated his contempt for the whole process by stomping off the porch and into the village, not even bothering to stay for the discussion. Osman thought he would be forced to insist that Murad leave so he could speak to the wife privately, but then Murad no doubt knew just how frustrating a conversation with her could be and decided to leave the policeman to it.

'So, *Mak Cik*,' he began with a smile he hoped inspired confidence, 'have you heard about what happened to *Mak Cik* Maryam?'

She regarded him quietly, but did not respond. She was small and pale, with steel-grey hair and wire-rimmed glasses. She seemed stooped and old, but when he thought about it, she was probably no older than Maryam and Rubiah, who seemed years younger and infinitely more energetic. She seemed to be melting into the background whenever he took his eyes off her, and perhaps she'd perfected that trick in order to stay out of Murad's way.

'You know *Mak Cik* Jamillah has passed away.'

She smiled slightly. He took it as a 'yes'.

'*Mak Cik* Maryam is helping us with the investigation,' he told her. 'You met her, right?' Again, she smiled. 'And now she's been attacked.'

'Really?' she whispered.

'Yes!' he said, encouraged. 'This was, let me see ... about five days ago. We've been asking everyone where they were last Thursday night.'

'Good!' she said softly.

'And where were you?' he prompted.

'With my son, Kamal,' she said, so softly he could hardly hear her.

'Ah. Where?'

'Kamal? Why, he lives here, of course! With us. He's captain of his own boat now.' She leaned closer to Osman, as though to impart something particularly important. 'It's about time he got married. I'm looking for a nice girl for him.'

She leaned back and smiled, as though she expected congratulations on her plans. As though every mother in Malaysia didn't feel exactly the same way. No wonder Murad had walked away, if he had conversations like this with her every day. It's a wonder it didn't drive him mad as well.

Osman smiled at her and said goodbye, leaving her sitting on the porch with the smile still on her face.

Only when she was sure he'd left, and no one else could see her, did she relax. The smile disappeared, her eyes became alert again, and she leaned against the roof posts, looking out towards the sea, considering what she'd just found out.

Chapter XIV

The trap was set at the market. Ashikin asked Rosnah to stop in and pick up some cloth there, ostensibly a gift to her mother. Azmi was coming to help his mother on her second day back at work. It was a godsend, really; working to get Azmi married had distracted the women of the family completely. Maryam stopped worrying about the case, Aliza about her hair. They were all locked in strategy for bringing the couple together while Azmi was in Kota Bharu.

Maryam now concentrated her energies on directing Azmi to accidentally run into Rosnah. As he ambled through the market carrying some stock, Ashikin grabbed his arm and swung him around to face Rosnah, introducing them

'Rosnah! Do you remember my brother Azmi?' she trilled, avoiding Azmi's eyes. 'You haven't seen each other for ages. Azmi's on leave from the army!' Ashikin then grabbed the package and called, 'Excuse me! I've got to help' and disappeared.

Rosnah smiled shyly at Azmi. 'She's really busy,' she said of Ashikin. 'How long are you back for?'

Azmi admired her smile. 'Just a few days on leave. I'm

stationed in Kok Lanas.'

'Oh, not too far,' she replied, twisting her handbag slowly. 'Well, I hope you enjoy yourself at home.'

Azmi smiled back at her. 'Yes, I am, though this' – he gestured at the hubbub – 'is a bit crazy.'

She nodded and agreed. 'Yes, but it's how we make a living, isn't it?'

He kept smiling. She excused herself and ducked away, not wanting to prolong her first meeting with him. Though she hadn't been told, she knew the introduction was not random. She was of an age where everyone was trying to find her a husband, and any man to whom she was properly introduced was a prospect.

* * *

Osman met his Thai counterpart at the border town of Sungei Golok, across the river from Kelantan. He'd brought Zainab with him, in case they actually found Zaiton; as her older sister, no doubt she had some influence over the girl and would help bring her back. Rahim he would handle himself.

The Thai policeman, whose name he stumbled over every time he tried to say it, seemed bored and removed from the project. His Malay was non-existent and his English spotty, so communication between the two was difficult. Luckily, however, Rahim's family had finally disgorged information on their relatives here, and he had the name of the *kampong*. He also had Zainab to speak Kelantanese if necessary – the dialect in this very Malay part of Thailand was even thicker, if that was possible, than in Kelantan.

They were driven through Sungei Golok, the neighbourhood Sodom, where all manner of sin existed, many of which did not – or were not supposed to – exist in Kelantan.

During the day, it looked like any other market town, with stalls sprawling throughout, packed with Thai goods ranging from durian (the 'durian Bangkok' widely believed to be the best variety ever) to kitchenware. In the evening, it would shimmer with lights: neon for the bars, strings of Christmas lights for the brothels, bare light bulbs and paraffin lanterns illuminating the night market.

The *kampong* in question was more utilitarian and a bit more run down than those in Kelantan, with houses closer together and less effort spent on flowers and keeping the yards clean.

Osman showed a picture of Rahim to everyone they met, asking if they knew where he was. Most of the villagers were wary of the police, and even warier of turning someone in to them, and it appeared that no one had seen him, or knew of him, or anyone related to him.

This area, Osman realized belatedly, was considered a hotbed of separatist activity, its inhabitants anxious to leave Thailand and join, or rejoin, their fellow Malays in Malaysia. They'd probably seen a good deal of the Thai police in recent years, and had learned to stay as far away as possible.

Zainab, however, had broken away from officialdom and had gone on her own to ask, telling everyone that she was looking for her younger sister who had run away from home with Rahim and how much she wanted her back. This, at last, was something everyone could understand, and Zainab was taken to the home where both Zaiton and Rahim were staying.

Zaiton greeted her with open-mouthed shock. 'How did you find me?'

'I had to come all the way here to look for you! What do you think you're doing?'

'I'm here with Rahim!' she answered defiantly.

Rahim sought to defuse the situation. 'It isn't what you think, *Kakak*,' he told her.

'Really? What do I think?'

'That I meant to, you know...' he blushed and looked uncomfortable. 'Because I didn't.'

'We're married!' Zaiton announced proudly.

'What?' Zainab screeched.

Rahim's relatives gathered around her to calm things down, several explaining at once that Rahim's intentions were entirely honourable, and marriage was a respectable state, and they had witnessed it, and it was all legal. They had even given a small *kenduri,* a wedding feast to celebrate the occasion, so that Zainab would see this was no backstreet abduction, but a real and official wedding. Congratulations were in order!

Zainab took a firm hold of her sister's blouse and steered her rather roughly into a bedroom, pushed her on the bed and stood in front of her, arms akimbo, chin thrust forward and patience exhausted. 'Start talking,' she ordered.

'We're married,' Zaiton said firmly, but her defiance was already melting away. She twisted her hands, and then looked imploringly up at her. 'I had to, *Kakak*. I'm having a baby.'

Zainab suspected this might be the case from the moment

Zaiton had gone missing. '*Astaghfirullah*,' she moaned. 'How could you?'

'*Mak* knew.' Zaiton now began crying, but found absolutely no sympathy. 'I told her, just before the *main puteri*.'

'Our poor mother was already sick, needing to be cured, and you dropped this in her lap?'

'I had to tell her, so she would understand. She said we would organize the wedding right after the ceremony. She said she was sure she would feel better afterward, and be ready to help me. I know she was angry, but not *that* angry. She understood.'

'Understood?'

'I know it was a mistake, really, I do. But now it's been made good. I'm married, we're in love,' – here Zainab rolled her eyes and considered slapping her – 'and it will be fine. I'm not very far ...'

'Everyone will know anyway,' Zainab informed her. 'Running away to Golok to get married. People aren't stupid, you know. Just you,' she added under her breath.

Now it was Zaiton's turn to stick out her chin. 'I don't care. I'm married now. Rahim's parents know. We can live with them for a while.'

'And leave *Ayah* all alone at a time like this?'

'Well,' she said doubtfully, 'I guess we can stay with him if he'd like. I'm afraid he won't want us. But I'd like to stay with *Ayah* if I could. I could help at *Mak*'s stall, we can do it together.' She smiled tremulously, on the verge of crying again.

Zainab could see the advantage in that. Of course the two of them could take over their mother's business, it was only right as daughters that they do so. And if Zaiton and Rahim lived with their father, he wouldn't be lonely. When the baby came, he'd be with his grandchild and would no doubt love that. He'd get used to the fact that Zaiton (idiot!) had run away to get married – at least she'd gotten married.

Still, she deserved some punishment. Zainab suddenly leaned over and gave her foolish younger sister a hard smack across the face. Zaiton gasped and cried, holding her hand up to her cheek.

'That's for getting pregnant before you were married. You know better than that! We'll make the best of it, we have to and we will. But aren't you ashamed?'

She nodded silently, tears rolling down her cheeks. 'I am. I'm ashamed I worried *Mak* the way I did. And now *Ayah* too, and you. I've been terrible.' She cried into her hands.

'Oh, stop it,' Zainab said tiredly, her mind already running over how to put it to their relatives and neighbours in the best possible light. She wondered if, according to religious law, the child would still be considered illegitimate. Maybe, but once it arrived, everyone would probably forget how it was conceived and Zaiton would be just another young wife and mother.

She'd missed out on a wedding, which every girl looked forward to. The *bersanding*, the sitting-in-state in the splendour of *songket*, with attendants fanning the new couple, the highlight of every wedding, would never be hers. But that was her choice, and she'd have to live with it. Maybe they could get a picture taken of them in rented finery so they'd have something to show their children.

'Come on.' Zainab yanked her arm and pulled her to her feet.

In the living room, everyone looked relieved when the two came out. It was clear that everything would be alright. Even though Rahim's relatives knew the whole story, Zainab was reluctant to tell it to Osman with a full audience, and she pulled him, together with the young couple, over to a corner of the room. The rest of the family tactfully withdrew outside, or into the kitchen, to give them some privacy.

Osman's face creased with concern as he heard the story. Would it be a motive to kill Zaiton's mother? If she already knew, and Zaiton was telling the truth, then there was no reason. However, if her story was now a convenient whitewashing of the truth, then it might certainly push one or the other, or both together, to murder. Still, Osman could not bring himself to consider that this girl would kill her own mother. It was unnatural, and he hated to even consider it. He looked at them both, trying to divine from their eyes whether they could really be that wicked. He wanted to see that it was impossible, but the policeman in him wouldn't allow it.

Chapter XV

Though back at the market, Maryam was still not herself. She tried to think about the case, but her mind was still blurred, and she became easily tired and even more easily irritated. Mamat had suggested she stay away from the market for a while: 'Let Ashikin handle the stall – you know she'll do a great job.'

Maryam erupted in fury. He'd never seen her like that, and everything he said in an attempt to pacify merely seemed to stoke her rage. He tried to keep the children out of her way. Aliza was still delicate, and needed tender care. He worried about her. Whenever he looked at her, without her curly hair, her eyes huge in her face, he cursed himself for not protecting her, for not protecting all of them.

Yi was home now, and just a kid, and frightened by this new side of his mother. He sent them both to stay with Maryam's brother Malek and his family, confident they would be comfortable while Maryam had a rest, while he could devote his time to her recovery. After all, without her in the centre of the family, everything would fall apart.

He tried to talk to Maryam as she prepared dinner, hoping to draw her out. She was pale lately, and haggard. Really, she should have been resting, but she refused. Rubiah tried to bring dinner over every night, but Maryam wouldn't have it, and Rubiah would leave without comment.

Maryam squatted on the floor of the kitchen, chopping onions and garlic with a will so vicious Mamat flinched every time her knife hit the board. 'So, what have you heard about the case?'

The knife hit even harder, threatening to break the board.

'The case,' she answered bitterly. 'Well, Zaiton ran away to Sungei Golok to get married to Rahim. I understand she's having a baby. Her poor mother.'

Whack! The onions were already pulverized and she put them in a pan to fry. Now she brought out a coconut grater and began using it. Bits of coconut were spraying around the kitchen. He feared she would hurt herself, but knew if he said anything, she'd probably throw the whole thing in his face.

'Now, would a daughter kill her own mother so she could get married sooner? It's unnatural. And I thought Rahim was a nice boy, but now I'm not so sure.' She began squeezing out the milk from the grated coconut, with a gusto which made it look like she was strangling someone.

'And you know what else I think? That wife of Murad is crazy. All her answers are like a code, if only I could figure it out.' She stopped for a moment, and reflected.

'There's something wrong there. Though, of course, being married to Murad could probably make anyone crazy.' She resumed throttling the coconut.

* * *

Mamat made the trip to Bacok while Maryam was busy at the market, so she wouldn't know he'd gone. Rubiah had also urged him to go to *Pak* Nik Lah, and ask what could be done for her. Perhaps Maryam needed a *main puteri* as well – something was changing her, and it wasn't healthy. Mamat prayed the *bomoh* could give him some hope of a cure; he was out of ideas, and felt increasingly helpless watching his wife sink further into unhappiness.

Pak Nik Lah greeted him with professional courtesy, and Mamat could see immediately why people trusted him with their problems. He was grave, yet easy to talk to, infinitely sympathetic, yet practical too. Without making a conscious decision to do so, Mamat unburdened himself completely, telling him all that had happened and why. The *bomoh* offered him a cigarette, his wife laid out coffee and fried bananas, and for the first time since the attack, Mamat felt a solution might be found.

Pak Nik Lah leaned over, elbows resting on his knees, his eyes kind.

'It's a great burden for her, I can feel that,' he told Mamat. 'She came to see me, with her cousin, was it? And I thought then, what a brave woman! And smart, too, I could see that.'

He sighed, and took a drag on his cigarette. 'Often it's the people who are the smartest who suffer the most, you see. Other people don't notice things, or they don't always know what things might mean. But someone like your wife, she'll take it all in. She can't pretend she doesn't know. And then, too, she's used to running things.' He smiled at Mamat in brotherhood, and Mamat could not help smiling back.

'My wife's the same. And then, when she feels she's fallen down on the job, she's very hard on herself.' He leaned back against the cushions, and took a sip of coffee.

'Spending time thinking about murder, it can't help but upset you. Your energy, your *semangat,* it's bound to be badly affected, and I'm afraid that's what may have happened. She's open to bad influences, and perhaps some *jinn* has taken advantage of that. It's made her angry, or rather, I should say, it's the *jinn* you're hearing when she's angry, not her. The cure would be to get rid of these influences, these *jinn*, so her own soul can come back in balance.'

'And how ...?'

'A *main puteri*, I would think.'

Mamat looked glum. 'I don't see her wanting the whole *kampong* attending something like that. She'd be uncomfortable.'

They sat silent for a moment. 'We could try to do a small one,' the *bomoh* suggested, a touch doubtfully. 'I can think about it. I see what you mean, but you need the music and all that. You can't do it quietly.'

'I see.' He really did, but feared bringing it up to Maryam.

'Let me come and talk to her,' advised *Pak* Nik Lah. 'Let's see what we can do.'

Mamat agreed fervently. 'Yes, let's. Tomorrow? I'll try to get her home from the market early.' He wrung *Pak* Nik Lah's hand gratefully, and walked down the stairs feeling better, hopeful that now it was possible to have things improve, and maybe everything would indeed turn out right.

The next afternoon saw *Pak* Nik Lah at their house, with Rubiah, Ashikin, Malek and Aliza in attendance for moral support. Maryam served coffee and snacks, cigarettes were passed around, and *Pak* Nik Lah smiled encouragingly. Maryam looked, and felt, suspicious and uncomfortable. Something was up.

'*Kakak*, I've heard about your injury, and yours, *Mek*,' he smiled at Aliza, who smiled shyly back, 'and I'm sorry for it.' Maryam murmured something polite but unintelligible.

'I see you're tired and tense. I don't think that's like you.' Maryam shot Mamat a look, but said nothing. 'Such a strain you've been under lately: investigating murder, which is bound to upset anyone, and then this terrible attack. It's no wonder you've been nervous.

'And, of course, *Kakak*, being nervous, you've been weakened. It happens all the time. I'm so sorry to see you suffering.'

'I'm fine,' she said curtly, rubbing her hands on her sarong.

He smiled at her again. 'Those close to you are worried about you. They can see how you're trying to be strong for your family, but they can be strong for you, too. They can help you. You don't need to bear it all by yourself.'

Maryam watched him warily. The others watched Maryam.

'Perhaps there is something we can do to ease the pressure on you, *Kakak*. To make you feel more like yourself.'

'*Adik*,' Malek said softly, 'I'm worried about you. You're too thin, too tired. You've been through too much. I feel I must do something.'

'About what?' she answered quietly. 'What can you do?'

'A cure. A clearing of your heart of this trouble. A rest for your injury, and for Aliza.'

'Absolutely,' Rubiah chimed in. 'This has been so difficult for you. Such an injury! Such a case!'

Maryam looked slowly around the circle of her family. 'You all believe this?'

They nodded – even Aliza, frail as she still was.

To Mamat's consternation, and the surprise of everyone else, Maryam began to cry: heavy sobs which seemed torn out of her. They crowded around her, stroking her arm, her back, her hair; assuring her it was alright to cry, and she need not be strong always.

They urged her to let them help her, to regain her strength and her equilibrium. It could be done; hadn't *Pak Cik* Lah done it for others? And weren't they much better afterwards than they had been? To regain one's peace of mind was the main thing, and then Maryam could continue on as she had been – the mainstay of her family, an admired businesswoman and the saviour of the Kota Bharu Police Department.

Rubiah wiped Maryam's face with a cold, wet cloth when she had stopped crying, and Ashikin sat behind her to rearrange her hair. Mamat looked relieved as he held her hand, and Malek beamed and held Aliza in his lap, though she was really too tall for that. *Pak* Nik Lah smiled beneficently upon them all.

'A *main puteri*, *Kakak*, that's what we'll do. You know, when you lose your balance, so to speak, *jinn* can invade you and they'll make you miserable. When you're restored, the *jinn* leave. They don't have a chance.' A soft giggle passed around the group, as much for relief as anything else.

'When can we do it?' Rubiah asked.

Pak Nik Lah thought. 'We will do it for both *Kakak* Maryam and *Mek* Aliza,' he smiled.

'My hair!' Aliza burst out.

'I know,' he said kindly. 'We'll wait a bit so you're stronger. But you must promise me, *Kakak*, you will eat, and you will rest, or you won't be strong enough.' He suddenly looked stern.

Maryam sniffed and blew her nose. 'I will.'

'Excellent.' He stood up. 'I am so glad. I know this will succeed.' He said his goodbyes, and left with Mamat to make arrangements.

Everyone else clustered about her, talking excitedly. Rubiah got to her feet and announced she was going home to cook.

'And you'll eat it,' she warned Maryam. 'No more arguments!' She held up her hand as if to ward them off, but Maryam said nothing.

'And I'm taking over the stall, every morning at least,' Ashikin announced. Arrangements had already been made for Rubiah's daughter Puteh to help out as well. 'And don't argue with me either,' she warned.

'I think you're all taking advantage of this to order me around,' Maryam grumbled, but she, too, was deeply relieved. She was loathe to admit it, but her sudden rages frightened even her, and she worried about her inability to focus on the case. And even though no cure had yet been done, just agreeing to it made her more confident. She would rest, she would eat, and she would find the murderer. *Jinn* or no *jinn*.

Chapter XVI

Osman sat stiffly on the bus from Kota Bharu to Ipoh. It left at night, so passengers could sleep through most of the 14-hour ride, although in Osman's case, this was more hope than possibility. He had been afraid about leaving while Maryam was ill, and had postponed coming home, which infuriated his mother.

'We have so much to do here!' she scolded him. 'Weddings don't happen in a day!'

Though he explained why he couldn't leave just yet, she refused to be mollified. 'Are you the only person on the whole police force?' she asked.

Even upon hearing what had happened to Maryam, she remained unmoved, and threatened to come to Kota Bharu and drag Osman home. He actually worried she would do that, humiliating him in front of his men. But thankfully, she had too much to do at home, as she told him; otherwise she'd be there.

He thought Maryam now seemed to be improving. Mamat told him about the *main puteri* to come, and though he was surprised Maryam agreed to it, he felt strongly that she needed it. Now he believed he could leave for a little while to get married, without the whole investigation falling apart. Between Rahman and Maryam, neither at full capacity, but together still formidable, he felt sure things would go well. Especially with those two backed up by a newly invigorated Rubiah.

He felt lighter than he had in months, as though the weight of the job, and of the foreign soil of Kelantan, had lifted from him. He would be home soon, where the smallest mumbled comment would be instantly understood and no one would look to him for advice or orders. His mother would not even look to him for agreement – she would expect her own orders to be followed, and quickly. He sighed with contentment.

He saw his father waiting as the bus pulled into Ipoh. He was a mild-mannered man, accustomed to agreeing immediately with his wife rather than undergoing hours of futile wrangling, and he and Osman understood each other.

Standing with him, with his suitcases at their feet, Osman looked around at the busy street, proprietarily proud of Ipoh's commercial bustle. It was bigger and more energetic than Kota Bharu, and more cosmopolitan, too. He threw back his shoulders and straightened his spine: he was proud to be from Perak – and he was no foreigner here!

His mother eyed him critically when he entered the house.

'Look who's here!' his father cried jovially, beaming as though he had personally whisked Osman home from Kelantan. His two younger sisters bounced around him, inexplicably having suddenly matured into marriageable young women.

'You look thin,' his mother, Asmah, commented. 'Don't they feed you there?'

Osman almost asked who 'they' were, who were responsible for him, but stifled himself quickly, giving her a slightly embarrassed smile. 'Oh, I eat fine,' he assured her.

She sniffed. 'Then why are you thin? Anyway,' she continued, 'There's plenty of food here for you. You must have missed good Perak food up there.'

'Of course, he did,' his father slapped him affectionately on the back. 'Sit down and eat!'

His family all sat down and regarded him closely, as though they weren't sure he still knew how to eat. They waited expectantly, gauging his reaction to his native cuisine, and he did not disappoint.

'*Laksa*!' he cried, digging in enthusiastically to the soupy noodle-and-sour curry mixture. 'Real *laksa*. I've missed it so much! In Kelantan, it's very sweet, and thick, not like this.' He took a large spoonful and looked blissful. 'Oh, not like this at all.'

Relieved and happy chatter broke out around him; the wanderer had returned, carried back by *laksa*.

* * *

His mother had Osman recumbent on the couch in the living room. He had changed into his sarong and T-shirt, and was paralyzed by the amount of food he had eaten. He fought to keep his eyes open and pay adequate attention to what his mother was telling him. He knew from experience there would be a test later.

'You remember her,' his mother stated, brooking no disagreement. '*Mak Cik* Nah's husband's sister's daughter … she was at your grandmother's party a couple of years ago.'

Osman struggled to look thoughtful, but could bring to mind no memory other than the photo his mother had sent him. He concentrated on it and tried to flesh it out with a personality, but the only one which came to him was his mother's.

'Can you get her a job teaching in Kota Bharu? You're the police chief, after all, and you must have influence.' His mother leaned back and regarded him. 'Are you listening to me?'

He nodded dutifully.

His mother smacked him on the leg with a newspaper. 'Alright, Man. Now tomorrow, we have to get your wedding outfit ready. Cream is the wedding colour - pay attention! We'll go to the tailor, and then we'll get the waistcloth to match.'

'I have one,' Osman mumbled. 'This lady in Kota Bharu gave it to me.'

'Who?'

'The one who helped me with the murder, *Mak Cik* Maryam. She sells *kain songket* in the market. This is really top quality …'

His mother sniffed. 'We'll see. Does it match cream?'

Osman didn't know how to answer. *Match cream? Doesn't everything?* He dared not ask. 'Yes, I'm sure …'

His mother rose. 'Go to sleep, you look tired. Tomorrow morning, we'll go.' She swept out of the living room, leaving Osman already half-asleep (a purely protective measure), relieved to know you *can* go home again.

Chapter XVII

Weddings were in the air. Since her mother had given up the reins, if only temporarily, Ashikin felt the responsibility devolved to her. It was time to get Azmi in gear: he did not really seem reluctant to move forward with Rosnah, but was certainly in need of a push, and she was just the one to give it to him. She called him at his army camp, using the phone in Daud's parents store, and after several tries, finally got him on the line.

'Azmi! It's me, Ashikin.'

'What's up? Is something wrong? Is everyone alright?'

'Fine. *Abang*,' she said, getting quickly down to business (no point in spending money on a phone call about nothing). 'Did you like Rosnah? My friend?'

'I remember who she is,' he answered a mite testily. 'She seemed nice.'

'Well, nice enough that *Mak* and *Ayah* should talk to her parents? Or not that nice?'

'I don't know.'

'Azmi,' she said patiently, 'don't start sulking.'

'I'm not!'

'You are,' she said, unruffled. 'But that's OK. If you're interested, we should do something pretty soon. It's been a while. If not, tell me and I'll let it go.'

'I'd like to see her again once more before I say anything.'

'When?'

'*Adik*! I've got to get leave and everything. I can't work on your schedule!'

'Get leave, then.'

Ashikin was a veteran of many negotiations with Azmi, and knew the trick was not to get riled no matter what the provocation. He would soon calm down.

'*Adik*!' he repeated.

'OK,' she replied. 'Just get leave for a day and I'll arrange for us all to meet. That's all you need. Otherwise,' and now she brought out the stick, having exhausted the carrot, '*Mak* is going to start looking for girls on her own, and then you can talk to her and not me.'

It was a real threat. Ashikin could be reasoned with; their mother was a different breed altogether. Azmi might well find himself married before he quite knew what had happened.

'I'll see when I can get leave. I thought she was nice,' he said, calming down as his sister knew he would. 'Pretty, too. I'll call the store as soon as I know. Maybe we should all three have lunch? No – Daud, too. Make it four, OK?'

'OK,' she replied, satisfied with the result of her call. 'Let me know and I'll take it from there.'

She told Daud of the conversation that evening over dinner. 'So, we'll all meet for lunch,' she concluded, 'as soon as Azmi gets a day's leave. I should check this out with Rosnah, don't you think? Make sure she liked him.'

Daud nodded absently.

The next morning, Ashikin hopped on to the back of Daud's motorbike, and they set out for Kedai Buluh, on the road to the beach where the Kelantan River ran into the sea. The village was dense with thickets of bamboo, and close enough to the ocean that the soil turned sandy. Ashikin always enjoyed coming here, where her beloved uncle Malek lived.

While Kampong Penambang was also green when you left the main road into the maze of houses, yards and trees, it was more populated than Kedai Buluh, and there were gaps in the trees where houses sat, making room for the sun to fall on the swept, flat yards. Kedai Buluh had fewer houses and more gaps between the trees, along with an unbroken view of the Kelantan River as it headed to the South China Sea, stretching cool and blue to the horizon.

Rosnah's family owned a small *budu* factory, and made a variety of products from dried fish as well: *keropok,* puffy fried shrimp and fish chips; *ikan bilis,* dried anchovies sold as a condiment; and, of course, *budu*, a delectable fish sauce. The grounds were busy at mid-morning, with several women flattening dried fish in preparation for putting proto-budu out to ferment, and some men carrying large containers of fish. The smell was strong but not overpowering, as the sea breeze freshened the air.

Ashikin walked into the small wooden building serving as an

office while Daud wandered around outside, leaving his wife to undertake the delicate negotiations with her friend.

'Rosnah!' Ashikin greeted her as she walked in the door. 'How are you?'

'Fine, fine,' she answered, rising from behind the desk. 'Just doing the invoices, you know. Come and sit down. Coffee, soda?'

'Soda, thanks. It's getting hot.'

Rosnah walked over to a small fridge, took out two Green Spot orange sodas for them, and poured them into glasses.

'So,' she began, 'what's up?'

'Just stopping by, see how you're doing,' said Ashikin with studied indifference.

Rosnah leaned over, laughing at Ashikin. 'Kin, everyone I know is trying to match me up. Everywhere I go, there's always some guy who happens to be there, who I happen to be introduced to. It's always an amazing coincidence. So, are you also in the marriage market?'

Ashikin grinned back at her. At least she seemed amused, and not angry. 'Ros, come on. I'm embarrassed as it is.'

'So, I'm right.'

'Sort of.'

'Your brother.'

'Azmi. Yes. What did you think?' she asked boldly. *Well*, she told herself, *the secret was already out, so there wasn't any point in playing coy*.

'Seems nice.'

'That's all?'

'What does that mean?'

'I'm trying to be very discreet here!' Ashikin complained. 'I'm trying to ask you this without anyone getting upset.'

'I'm not upset,' Rosnah seemed genuinely surprised. 'I'm just asking. You're my friend, not some *Mak Cik* I don't know, so why shouldn't I ask you?'

'OK. You can ask me.'

'What does that mean?' she repeated patiently.

'It means,' Ashikin took a deep breath, 'would you welcome any further interest, or would you rather wait?'

'Ah. You mean a visit to my parents?'

'Maybe. I'm just asking to see how you feel. This isn't official or anything.'

'OK, it's unofficial; then, let me see. Well, he's nice.'

'Would you like to have lunch, the four of us? That way you can see him again without having to commit to anything.'

Rosnah nodded. 'That could work. Just exploratory, right?'

'Right.'

'Yes, great. Let's do it.'

'I thought maybe a *satay* breakfast on a Friday.'

'Perfect.'

The two smiled at each other, pleased with the arrangements they'd made. 'Great!' said Ashikin enthusiastically. 'Well, I'll let you get back to your work. I'll be by as soon as I know a day when he's coming back.'

'Thanks, Kin.' Rosnah waved goodbye. 'Daud, hi!' He waved back at her as he swung his leg over the motorbike.

'Hi!' he called, waiting for Ashikin to climb aboard. With that, they drove away down the road, while Rosnah stood for a few moments, watching them go.

* * *

Aziz, following Zainab's advice, gave a *kenduri* for Zaiton and Rahim to celebrate their wedding. All the families in Kampong Penambang attended, or at least sent representatives, so it was counted a great success and social event.

Maryam approved. If Aliza, God forbid, was ever in such a situation (the very thought made her feel faint), then that's exactly what she would do.

No one was fooled. Why else would they have run away to get married in Sungei Golok instead of having a real ceremony at home? Of course, it would have been unseemly to do it so soon after her mother died, and therefore it was clear that time was of the essence. Which led everyone to the correct conclusion.

Nevertheless, by the time the baby arrived, most people would be hazy about how much time had actually elapsed, while those who were clear about it would never say anything, and the whole thing would fade away. Zainab consoled her father with the fact that two years from now, no one would even remember there hadn't been a wedding here in Kelantan – they'd remember the *kenduri* and that would be enough.

It was excellent advice and followed to the letter. After the celebration, the young couple moved in with Aziz and kept him company. He found himself counting the days until his grandchild's arrival, no matter what its inception had been.

* * *

Rest was the order of the day in Kampong Penambang. Maryam had been convinced to take several days off, leaving the business to Ashikin, and she admitted it had helped a great deal. Rubiah had been catering all the meals, refusing to allow her cousin near the kitchen. New platters of cakes, in tempting assortments, arrived daily. If necessary, Rubiah would stand over them until every last one was eaten.

Both Aliza and her mother filled out a little and lost some of the drawn and hunted look they had earlier. To help them mend, Mamat often brought their favourite foods home, as well as candy, and although Maryam didn't necessarily agree with it as a healthy choice, she did not have the energy to argue or to spoil Mamat's pleasure in spoiling them.

Aliza checked the mirror several times an hour to see if her hair had grown in, and indeed, there was a crop of very short fuzz now covering her scalp. Her parents found it very comforting; it had been difficult for them both to see her bald and fragile.

* * *

Maryam's mind had not been still while she was at home, though Rubiah had refused until now to be drawn into any discussion of the case. Today, however, Maryam felt it was time, and insisted she listen. Rubiah watched over the tops of her eyeglasses, as she quietly picked out Maryam's favourite cakes and pushed them toward her. These were not the custardy sort, they were much simpler (though no less sweet), and Rubiah approved the choice as a ladylike and appropriate one.

'There's one thing that bothers me,' Maryam began.

'Only one?' She rolled her eyes.

Maryam ignored the irony. 'Murad and his wife. Osman told me he spoke to her, but she didn't make a lot of sense. I think he wrote her off after that, but I'm not sure about that. I think she's craftier than everyone thinks, though I'm not saying she isn't crazy. But she isn't … harmless crazy.'

Maryam resolutely polished off two *onde-onde* cakes in quick succession to prove she was thinking hard and on top of her game. 'I'm not falling for it.' She then ate a third as a show of bravado, and considered a fourth. Why not? Everyone said she was too thin, and how long had it been since she'd worried about that? She couldn't remember.

Rubiah considered this. 'I think she's crazy, too,' she admitted. 'I haven't considered her at all, she's like a ghost.'

'Exactly. A ghost. No one sees what they're up to, ghosts.'

'What do you want to do?' Rubiah thought she knew what was coming.

'I think we should speak to Noriah again.'

'You shouldn't go out,' Rubiah said flatly.

'What if we got a car? I can call Rahman. I already feel as if I'm running the police department. Osman's off getting married, and they'll do whatever I tell them!'

'It's frightening,' Rubiah agreed.

* * *

Noriah was surprised to see Maryam, Rubiah, Rahman and a junior policeman coming into her yard. Maryam looked much thinner than she remembered her and wore a headscarf wrapped tightly to cover her forehead as well as her hair. She'd heard something about the attack – hadn't everyone in Kota Bharu? – but didn't expect to view the results firsthand.

She greeted them uncertainly: '*Kakak*!'

The two policemen melted away in search of a coffee stall. Maryam and Rubiah climbed the stairs to the porch slowly, so as not to tire out the patient. The pleasantries began, the food was served. Noriah was particularly solicitous towards Maryam, recognizing she was still weak.

'How are you?' she asked with concern.

Maryam shrugged as if to say it was nothing, and apologized for getting right to the point. She feared she would become tired and unable to carry on for too long, and wanted to ensure she asked all her questions in time.

'*Kakak*, I've been thinking about Hamidah, is it? Your brother's wife.'

Noriah sniffed in disapproval. 'She's a weak woman. Not really worthy of my brother.'

'How do you mean?'

'You've met her?'

Maryam nodded.

'So you can see, she's a bit ... off. Not really a partner for my brother. Though I really shouldn't say,' she began preening, 'since she's my daughter's mother-in-law now.'

Maryam and Rubiah looked around, and took in the bits of

decoration still hanging on the porch from the wedding: tinsel and a small, sparkling model of a palm tree in the corner. 'You've had a wedding here!' Rubiah cried, trying hard to inject enthusiasm into her voice.

'Yes, my daughter Hayati married her son Kamal. An excellent match. He's as good a man as his father!' Maryam thought it a completely ambiguous compliment, but Noriah clearly believed it was high praise indeed. 'They'll be very happy together.'

She now chattered happily, extolling the match and the work ethic of those involved. 'Of course, Kamal has a lot to do, running his own boat, it's quite a lot of responsibility. And Yati, she helps here. She works hard, very diligent. I'm proud of her.'

She beamed at her guests. 'They're living here now. Yati, you know, wanted to stay with her family for a while.' (*As opposed to living with Murad*, Maryam thought, *which would be hell on earth.)* 'But they'll be saving money ...'

'I'm sure they will,' interjected Rubiah sweetly.

Noriah gave her a sharp look, as though she suspected this was not uttered in perfect sincerity, but her own enthusiasm soon reasserted itself, and she continued. 'Yes, it's all we could have wished for.'

'His parents must miss him,' Maryam said mildly.

'Oh, he sees his father every day. Talks to him about the boat, you know. And he's a good boy, he remembers his mother.'

She leaned forward confidentially. 'My brother and I made these arrangements, you see. Hamidah, she couldn't pay attention. Never can. And I thought ... well, perhaps I shouldn't say this.' Maryam knew she would, anyway,

'I think Hamidah may have had an eye on Aziz's daughter. Can you imagine? The one who just got married in Sungei Golok? What was that, anyway?'

Maryam and Rubiah ignored the implication; they might condemn Zaiton at home, but in front of this woman, they closed ranks and refused to even acknowledge it might be out of the ordinary.

'She was interested in Zaiton then?'

Noriah was deprecating. 'Who knows? It's hard to know what she's thinking, that woman. But no matter, Murad would never allow it.'

'Would Aziz and Jamillah?'

She pursed her lips and looked hard at them, but apparently decided that no one could be more admiring of Kamal than she was herself, so she must have misunderstood. 'You're right.' Noriah agreed. 'They were a difficult family, Aziz and Jamillah. But it's all coming back to them.'

'Coming back?'

'Their daughter. You know.'

'I hear they're all very happy. The new couple is living with Aziz, to keep him company.'

'And I hear there's a baby coming.' Noriah looked smug.

'Well, isn't that what marriages are for?' Maryam smiled. 'I am so sorry, *Kakak*, but I'm afraid I must go. I still feel a bit weak you know.' Noriah stood up and began fluttering around Maryam.

'No, don't worry, I will be fine, and I'm so happy to have seen you! And to be able to wish you the best on the marriage! This is certainly the season for them, isn't it?'

They found Rahman lounging at the car, coffee in one hand and curry puffs in the other. He too looked quite content. He managed to hold the cup and curry puffs and open the car door with a flourish, all at once. 'It looks like you're mending faster than you thought,' she told him.

'Did you find out what you wanted?'

Maryam sighed, thrilled to be able to sit back in the car. She hadn't realized how quickly she tired nowadays, and with this lethargy came headaches. The mark of the *enam sembilan* began to throb, and she couldn't decide whether it was the heat, over-exertion, or Noriah's conversation. The last seemed most probable, but that may have been caused by the pain, which always put her in a bad mood.

'I don't know,' she finally answered, taking care not to be short with him: that was the way she ended up waiting for a *main puteri* in the first place. 'Her daughter's married Murad's son, and she seems delighted. I wonder if the daughter feels the same.'

'She's from the family. I don't know why you'd assume she wouldn't be just like her mother. *Susu didada tak dapat dielakkan:* there's no avoiding mothers' milk,' Rubiah pronounced solemnly.

'You don't even know her,' Maryam chided her.

'If you know the family, you know the child!'

'Rubiah!' Then, all of a sudden, Maryam closed her eyes.

'You're feeling sick again,' Rubiah announced. 'Rahman, let's get home as quickly as you can.'

Chapter XVIII

The day of the *satay* party arrived. Aliza begged to join them. 'See? My hair's started to grow in. It would be great for me to go out now!'

'You go out every day, to school. This is for grown-ups.'

'I won't do anything stupid,' Aliza announced. 'I just want to go!'

'Take her,' Mamat told her. 'She deserves to have some fun.'

Aliza was beside herself with excitement, and kept dancing around Daud. 'Do you think they'll like each other? I hope so. It would be great for Azmi, really. He needs some stability.'

Daud laughed at her. 'Stability? Where did you hear that?'

'*Mak*.'

'Your mother and sister just want to make sure he marries a Kelantan girl. They're afraid they'll have to entertain some Johor girl on the holidays and no one will know what she's talking about. Or worse yet, Azmi will go down to Johor for holidays!'

'You're right,' Ashikin agreed briskly. 'We've got to guard against it, and we are! How do I look?'

Daud looked her over. She looked, as always, lovely. She wore a nicely printed batik sarong, and a long, white lawn *baju kurung* over it. Her long hair was loosely bound at the back of her head, and her large brown eyes were shining.

'You're beautiful,' he said. 'You even know you're beautiful. Where's Azmi?'

'We're meeting him there. Hurry up!'

They entered a popular coffeeshop, which served *satay* on Thursday and Friday. The *satay* chef squatted outside the coffeeshop, under the roof covering the sidewalk in the manner of the Old West. Before him stood a small charcoal hibachi grill, which he fanned enthusiastically to keep the flames bright.

The uncooked *satay*, already seasoned and skewered, was laid out next to him on an oilcloth, in piles of chicken, beef and goat. A small boy at his side was in charge of the condiments: rice cakes, sliced cucumbers and a spicy peanut sauce. The boy arranged the cooked *satay* on a plate with the side dishes and served them in the shop.

It was Friday, the start of Kelantan's weekend, and after the men attended Friday services at the mosque, the shop was packed with families and groups of friends enjoying a *satay* brunch. Like all the Malay men there, both Daud and Azmi were decked out in traditional Malay clothing, which men wore to Friday services. The outfit consisted of a plaid sarong topped with a long *baju Melayu*, a Malay shirt, made from light cotton and solid-coloured, high-collared and long-sleeved, but long and loose to keep cool. They looked formal yet comfortable in the heat.

Ashikin and Daud picked their way through the tables to

the air-conditioned room upstairs. It was quieter and more conducive to conversation. Azmi already had a table, and was waiting nervously. Ashikin sat down with him to provide some last minute coaching and a pep talk, while Daud went downstairs to order their meal and look for Rosnah.

'*Abang*,' said Azmi's sister sternly, 'be talkative and charming. You can be, and now's the time. See how you feel about her, and let her get to know you. And be polite to her, ask her if she wants something to drink, or coffee.'

'I know how to talk to people, *Adik*. I'm not sitting here *macam itik mendengarkan guntur,* like a duck listening to thunder, with no clue what's going on. I'll be OK.

'Of course, you will,' Ashikin soothed him. *Let him get his sulk out of the way now,* she thought. *Then he'll be fine for* Rosnah. 'I just want to make sure everything's OK.'

'It is OK. Just stop worrying, alright? I won't embarrass you.' He smiled suddenly. 'I'm your *abang*, you know.'

Daud came into the room, followed by Rosnah. She was as pretty as Azmi remembered. She had a round, friendly face, with a small snub nose and a dimple high in her cheek. Her complexion was a smooth mocha, and her thick black hair was cut short, in a straight bob with long bangs. Her eyes sparkled as she said hello to Azmi, and without quite realizing it, he smiled as he stood to greet her.

Not too long into the lunch, Azmi made up his mind. He would marry Rosnah. He would start taking his life seriously. She was pretty, she was nice, and she was funny. He enjoyed being around her. More than that, he would find out after they were married.

Then too, she knew his sister, and they were friends. That was a big plus; she'd get along with his family, and she lived close by. Yes, the deal was made – at least as far as he was concerned.

He leaned over to Rosnah, and asked quietly, 'Ros, you know I'm in the army, don't you? In Kok Lanas?'

She nodded.

'Well, how do you feel about it? I mean, would you want to be with someone in the army, or would you rather settle here? The army moves around quite a lot, you know.'

She blushed, and looked down at her hands. 'Azmi, what are you asking me?'

He laughed, and took her hand. She started at the gesture, but did not remove it. 'I'm asking you to marry me.'

Rosnah looked into his eyes. Ashikin looked at them both while Daud tried to be tactful and leave the table for a moment. They needed privacy. He took Ashikin's hand, but she didn't respond. 'Ashikin,' he hissed, 'come with me *now.*'

She looked at him, surprised. She suddenly realized what was happening and hurried to rise with him and walk away. She grabbed the shoulder of Aliza, whose eyes were round with excitement. Neither Azmi nor Rosnah seemed to notice them.

'Did you see, *Kakak*?' Aliza demanded. 'It worked!' She began jumping up and down. 'I knew it would work!' she exulted. 'See, Daud, they're going to get married. *Mak* will be so happy!'

And so she would. Later that afternoon, when Azmi asked her, 'Why don't you and *Ayah* go to see Rosnah's parents? Arrange the wedding,' Maryam threw her arms around him and beamed. She felt stronger immediately.

'Mamat, listen! Azmi wants to marry Rosnah! *Alhamdulillah!* I'm so happy'

Yi, Aliza and Ashikin buzzed with excitement, and Ashikin added just a touch of smugness to her attitude. 'I told you,' she said proudly to her mother.

'You were so right,' Maryam enthused. 'How clever you were to think of it. Oh my goodness. Well, we'll have everything now: *Anak baik, menantu molek,* a good child and a pretty daughter-in-law.'

Mamat slapped Azmi on the back. 'This is great. Will you stay in the army?'

'I don't know yet.' Azmi was suddenly serious. 'Maybe we should open a business here. Maybe, I don't know, work with *Pak Long* Malek. I don't know yet.'

'Well, plenty of time to think about it,' Mamat assured him. 'Don't start worrying yet.'

Maryam began to plan. 'Kin, can you and Rosnah arrange a time for us to go over there? Rubiah and Abdullah should come too, don't you think?' She turned to Mamat, who agreed. 'And Ashikin and Daud, Aliza and Yi. What should I wear?'

This last comment was clearly not directed at Mamat, who had walked outside with Azmi and Yi so the men of the family could share each other's company. But Maryam and her daughters had to plan their wardrobes.

Chapter XIX

'I guess everyone's getting married now: Azmi and Osman, Zaiton and that poor Hayati. I feel so sorry for her! Murad and Noriah together, and Kamal, who we never met. But if Noriah thinks he's wonderful ...'

'You're worried for no reason,' Rubiah grumbled. 'She's probably never been happier.'

'Why don't we meet her?' Maryam suggested firmly. 'I can't help but think that family was more to do with this than anyone else.'

'I vote for Murad.'

Maryam tried to be patient. 'I know you do. But it can't just be the person we like least.'

Rubiah gave her a look which clearly conveyed 'indeed, it could be', but said nothing. 'Let's meet her then. Why not ask them both to come here? That way you can save your strength, and also not have to see Noriah. In your current weakened state, that could be dangerous.'

Maryam laughed, a sound heard far more rarely than it was before the attack. 'You're right. I'm tired. Bring them here.

And maybe ...'

'What?'

'More cake.'

* * *

Rahman was dispatched to pick up Kamal and Hayati, and brought them to Maryam's after dinner. Together with two other policeman and Mamat, Maryam and Rubiah sat quietly on the porch, listening to the conversation inside, trying to be discreet so as not to frighten their suspects. Aliza joined them, ever curious, but still frightened. She squeezed herself between her father and Rahman, protected from both sides.

Rubiah had been correct. Hayati was a younger version of her mother: proud and talkative, radiating self-satisfaction. She entered the house, greeted everyone politely and sat down on the couch, smoothing her sarong with a pleased look.

Kamal was tall and saturnine, with a serious, even scornful expression. He looked down at the offered coffee cup as though he hadn't ever seen one before and feared it might wet the carpet.

'I hope you don't mind us inviting you here. I find, since the attack, I become tired so quickly.' She sought any reaction at all to the mention of the attack, but found none. Kamal said nothing, but Hayati's chatter made up for both of them.

'I've heard, *Mak Cik*. Horrible what people will do. I'm shocked! Morals have certainly crumbled, wouldn't you say? We try to act as we should, to work hard and avoid trouble.

'My husband, you might know, is now the captain of his own

boat,' she said proudly, patting his knee. 'He works very hard. And if I may say so, his men all admire him, young as he is. They look up to him. Such a young captain; most of them could never have contemplated such responsibility at his age.'

'Did you take over the boat from your father?' Rubiah asked innocently, trying to remind Hayati that Kamal had hardly saved his own money to buy it.

'He did.' Hayati looked momentarily puzzled as to why anyone would mention that. 'And he's running it well. Discipline. You know, *Mak Cik*, that's what the others lack and what we have.'

Maryam hastened to interject, heading off an outburst by Rubiah. It was unimaginably rude for this young girl to lecture her elders on her husband's excellence. Rubiah may have been forced to listen to it from Noriah, but it was unlikely she would sit quietly for it from this puffed-up youngster.

'Can you help me with this?' Maryam asked. 'The night *Mak Cik* Jamillah died, poor soul, do you remember where you were?

'Not at the *main puteri*,' Hayati sniffed. 'We don't really believe in it. My mother always says people should pull themselves together instead of calling on *jinn* or spirits. You should only depend on yourself. It makes you strong.'

'Does it?' Maryam asked mildly. 'I'll remember that.'

Hayati clearly didn't know how to read the danger signs in her audience.

'So we wouldn't have been here. Not that we'd have any reason to be anyway. Our families don't get along that well. You know, *Pak Cik* Aziz had a big fight with my father. You must have heard.' She smoothed her sarong again, admiring the pattern. Rubiah's fuse appeared to be growing shorter by the moment.

'What about your mother?' Maryam asked Kamal.

He seemed surprised to be spoken to. 'My mother?'

'Yes, did she get along with *Mak Cik* Jamillah or not?'

'Well, naturally, she would support my father.'

'Were they ever friends?'

'She knew *Pak Cik* Aziz growing up.'

'Yes. But I asked about how she got on with *Mak Cik* Jamillah.'

'Well!' This was clearly a young man unused to being corrected. His nose rose higher into the air, his lips pursed ever tighter, and his shoulders tensed. Maryam thought he looked ready to punish them all like naughty schoolchildren. 'They weren't close, no. My mother keeps to herself. She had no reason to seek out friends like that.'

'Indeed.'

Kamal grew angry. 'She's a very delicate woman. She devotes herself only to her family. To my father and to me. She doesn't need to run around in the market like some.'

'Who are you talking about?' Rubiah asked, dangerously soft.

'Why, *Mak Cik* Jamillah! My father says she spent time in the market to gossip and to loaf. To talk to other men. That was perfect for *Pak Cik* Aziz,' he said. 'A lack of modesty. My father says if you act a certain way, then you are inviting certain things to happen to you.'

Outside on the porch, Mamat and Rahman sat perfectly still, expecting an explosion.

'Is that what you think of everyone in the market?'

Hayati first realized his mistake. 'Not everyone ...'

Maryam cut her off. 'I asked him.'

He floundered. 'Well, my father says ...'

'That *Mak Cik* Jamillah deserved what happened to her?'

'Not really.' He snapped his mouth shut as though he would never open it again. 'I didn't mean it that way.'

'Perhaps you felt that you would be the person to deliver what you think *Mak Cik* Jamillah deserves.' Maryam's head had begun throbbing again. These people were literally driving her crazy. 'Did you think that?'

'Me?' Now he looked frightened. 'No, I would never ... Why would I? I'm just telling you what we thought. You asked me that! Not that anyone would do anything.'

'How could you think such a thing, *Mak Cik*?' Hayati chimed in, looking nervous herself.

'How can you be so disrespectful of *Mak Cik* Jamillah? She was working, just like you say you do. How have you been raised?' Rubiah burst out, unable to hold back any longer. '*Kurang ajar!* Badly brought up! And you so proud of yourselves when you should be ashamed. How dare –'

At this juncture, Rahman charged into the room, anxious to avoid physical violence, which he felt might be mere moments away. 'I think it's time I brought these two people home, don't you?' he began hopefully.

'Wait a minute,' Rubiah ordered him. 'We're not finished yet.'

'You aren't?' Hayat squeaked. Maryam surmised it must have been one of the only times in her life where she did not look pleased with herself.

Maryam turned to Kamal. 'Your mother told the police she was with you on the night I was attacked. What does that mean?'

'Well, it means we were together ...'

'She wasn't asked *who* she was with, just *where* she was.'

He bristled. 'My mother never lies.'

'Then tell me, where were you?'

'I ... I don't remember.'

'But you remember being with your mother.'

'Yes,' he said slowly, afraid to commit himself to any one story.

'I ask you now, again, where were you? The night *Mak Cik* Jamillah was killed, and the night I was attacked. Where were you?'

'Are you accusing me of killing her? Of hurting you?'

'Not right now.'

'I can't remember. You're confusing me.'

'I have heard your family keeps a pelesit, and that's how you've gathered your money.'

Now he was angry. 'That's not true! I don't believe in such things anyway. And besides, it would be evil. How can you say that?' He turned to Rahman. 'Is she allowed to say such things?'

'It's just a question.'

'It's wrong. I won't discuss it.'

'I'm done,' Maryam said to Rahman. 'They can go home.' Sandwiched between Rahman and another policeman, who without touching them, still appeared to be leading them, they were escorted to the car without a word.

Maryam rubbed her forehead, trying to still the throbbing, but it wouldn't stop. She leaned back in her chair, and Rubiah went to fetch her some tea.

'You know, I never believed the pelesit story, and still don't. But after listening to him, I may be willing to change my mind. She took a long sip of tea and closed her eyes. 'And I apologize, Rubiah. You were absolutely right about that girl.'

Rubiah nodded quietly, her correct assessment was beyond discussion. 'I know,' she agreed. 'She's as bad as her mother. Worse, maybe, because she's still young. Can you imagine her at Noriah's age?' She walked into the kitchen with her eyes closed, trying to blot out the vision she had just conjured.

Chapter XX

Pak Nik Lah was preparing for the ceremony, as he always did: talking to the family, chatting with neighbours, and in this case, even speaking to the police about Maryam's role. Speaking to Maryam herself, he found the conversation turning more towards Jamillah, as Maryam peppered him with questions with far more determination than he approached her. Afterwards, he was amused to find that she was as skilled an interrogator as he, though admittedly their styles were quite different.

Pak Nik Lah took a far more avuncular, even passive role, encouraging his informants to speak at will, following the wanderings of their mind with interest. Maryam could appear either sweet and motherly, completely sympathetic, or stern and motherly, tolerating no evasions, demanding a straight answer. The *bomoh* was unused to being on the informant's end of the conversation and found he talked as much as anyone.

Maryam told him about her illness: the aftermath of a concussion, complicated by what appeared to be a rational fear of more attacks to come. She told him of her previous case, and the black magic, together with poison, which had been used against her. At that time, at least, she'd found the charm, and she was grateful it hadn't touched any of her children. But now, though the *enam sembilan* assault had been directed entirely at her, Aliza had been hurt in what Maryam considered a related act of violence.

'And I can't even find out who did it!'

'Do you have any ideas?' asked *Pak* Nik Lah gently. 'I'm sure you have your suspicions.'

She thought for a moment. *Pak* Nik Lah offered her a cigarette and she accepted it absently, took a deep drag, and started speaking slowly, as though just now putting into words what had been inchoate thought.

'I like Rahim. I do. He's a hardworking boy; well, a man really. And even though I can't condone what he and Zaiton did, at least no one else was hurt. During my last case, everyone I spoke to had second wives, and their first wives were miserable. Now Rahim, he did the right thing as soon as he could. But I wonder ...'

She stared off into the greenery. 'Is he protecting someone else?' she mused. 'Zaiton says she told her mother, who agreed to the marriage, but that doesn't mean much because I can't check it. But then,' she now argued for the other side, 'what else could Jamillah do? Forbid them to marry when her daughter was pregnant? Of course not!' she answered her own question. 'It's impossible. She'd allow them to marry, no, she'd *force* them to marry.

'Did Zaiton realize that? Well, she should have! She'd have no reason to fear her mother's refusal.'

'And Rahim no reason to protect her?'

'I doubt the two of them have ever discussed it,' she said morosely. 'He's in love with her; he'd do anything to keep her safe and happy, don't you think?'

'Me? I don't know anything about it.'

'Yes, you do,' Maryam corrected him. 'You spent time finding out about Jamillah and her family, and even Murad and his. You probably know the killer already; you just don't know you know.'

This was an interesting angle. He considered all he'd found out, trying to perceive it differently and see if a suspect jumped out at him. He leaned back against the wall and drank some more coffee in the companionable silence. Finally he said, 'I don't want to accuse anyone without evidence.'

'Just give me your impressions of the people. You have no idea how much that would help me.'

'I'll try,' he agreed, and then sat silent, gathering his thoughts.

'Jamillah, as I said, was troubled. I think she felt herself becoming less important to her family, with her children grown and Aziz preoccupied. It happens a lot at that age, I think. She worried Aziz would leave her, though I couldn't see any real reason why she thought so.

'He was worried about money, after that deal he had with Murad. I didn't ask about money details because it doesn't concern me.' He paused. 'She detested Murad, which is no surprise after what happened, and his wife as well. Jamillah thought she was faking her vagueness to cover up how jealous she was of her.'

'Why jealous?'

'Jamillah worked in the market, had freedom, had friends. She wasn't bossed around by her husband.'

'I should say not! She made most of the money, I'll bet.'

Pak Nik Lah smiled. 'Maybe. But she lived the way most women live here, I think. Murad would never let his wife work in the market, or socialize with friends. She lived a very lonely life, and Jamillah thought that made her spiteful. She knew about the *pelesit* they kept, and she said it was really Hamidah's, that she cared for it, and she sent it out against Jamillah to drain her spirit and make her as unhappy as Hamidah herself.'

'I didn't know that.'

'I wouldn't tell you if it wasn't to find her murderer.'

She nodded.

'Aziz knew Murad and Hamidah well, they'd all grown up together. I wondered if Jamillah thought Aziz still had feelings for her?'

'Still?'

The *bomoh* looked slightly pained. 'Apparently they had crushes on each other as kids, before he met Jamillah, and before her marriage to Murad was arranged. I don't think that means anything, and it hasn't since before they were both married. I did wonder if that would have led Murad to take advantage of him, maybe to get back at him for all those years ago.

'Whether Hamidah herself had anything to do with the sale of the boat and which investors were paid, I also don't know. Murad and Aziz had a fistfight due to the money argument, and I don't know if any of this was involved as well. Now that I've said that, I would add that if it did, it likely would have been from Murad's end rather than Aziz's.'

'But that was so long ago!'

'I know,' he sighed. 'But Jamillah mentioned it, so it was on her mind. Aziz laughed when I brought it up and said it was ridiculous. On the face of it, of course, it is, but that doesn't mean it won't drive people to do things. Crazier things have driven people to even worse acts.'

'I know that well enough!' She thought back on a killing based on grade school enmity.

'Murad ... well, I only spoke to him once. He wouldn't see me. He lectured me about how *main puteri* was useless, and I was taking money from people for nothing. He's an unpleasant man. I think he'd hurt people just to see them unhappy. He must be terrible to live with.'

Maryam fervently agreed.

'I didn't see any *pelesit*, mind you. I heard from several people that he had one and they'd seen it. Rahim said he even saw Murad feeding it blood on the boat ... but as I said, that's just what I heard. I can't say whether it's true or not.

'Zaiton and Zainab were concerned about their mother. Zaiton didn't say anything about the baby, and Jamillah never mentioned it either. Zaiton was more worried about herself than her mother, but given her age and her situation, I guess it's natural. Zainab is a grown woman with children of her own. She's a good person, a good daughter. I like her very much.

'I only spoke to Rahim briefly, and only because Zaiton talked about him. I thought they'd get married in the end. As you say, he seemed a hard-working man, one who was in love with her and was afraid he wouldn't be considered good enough.

'To answer your question about whether or not I can guess at the murderer, the answer is “I don’t know”. I don’t suppose I’m helping you too much.’

She silently agreed with him; his vocation was reading people, to quietly learn more about them than they ever intended to reveal. Surely now would be the perfect time to exercise that gift; yet she felt he held back. Nevertheless, nothing would be gained by accusing him of that, better to appear to accept his answers at face value.

‘That’s not true! Did you speak to Kamal or Noriah … or her daughter?’

He shook his head, and Maryam refilled his coffee cup. ‘Not really. Just a few minutes with Noriah, and she told me what a great family they were, and how they saved money.’

Maryam burst into giggles. ‘I heard the same speech!’

He smiled. ‘I didn’t meet Kamal, or her daughter.’ He finished the cup, and started another one. ‘I doubt I’ve clarified anything. I really don’t have any idea who it might have been.’

‘Do you think Murad would have hurt Jamillah just to get at Aziz?’

He considered it. ‘I don’t think Murad would be bothered by it. If he wanted to get at Aziz, he’d do whatever it took, and consider it the right thing.’

She smiled serenely. ‘You can’t imagine how much help you are. Come, have some more cakes. Rubiah made them just for you!’

Chapter XXI

Osman looked over at his wife in the chair next to him. She was dressed head to toe in Maryam's sumptuous fabric, the cream and gold shimmering in the lights strung behind them. He wore cream as well, with Maryam's *songket* waistcloth. Though his mother was not completely pleased with the fabric (only because she hadn't personally selected it), his bride seemed thrilled with it.

While he was no connoisseur of *songket* himself, despite Maryam's attempts to educate him, it did appear to be thicker and richer than almost any fabric he'd seen before. He felt he'd acquitted himself well in bringing it back from Kota Bharu, no matter what his mother said. Most importantly, his new wife seemed to agree.

The legalities had been completed, they were officially married, and now they sat in two decorated chairs on a raised dais in the bride's home for the *bersanding*, the sitting-in-state. Dressed in their finery, staring straight ahead with their hands flat on their knees, they were fanned by two of their young cousins, also dressed up and very impressed with it.

One of the little girls had to be continually nudged to fan, for she was distracted by the *songket* skirt she wore, in particular how the gold seemed to wink in and out of existence.

The house was decorated so that hardly any space was bare of either draped tinsel, *songket* bunting, or twinkling lights strung across the walls. Pictures had been taken which would grace the walls of their house for the rest of their lives together, and now they tried to keep solemn faces, though their friends tried their best to make them laugh. Both Osman and Azrina, his wife, were exhausted, but the wedding night lay ahead of them and they would both admit to a bit of trepidation.

Azrina would be accompanying Osman back to Kota Bharu, where she hoped to find a place as a maths teacher, which she was here in Perak. If the prospect frightened her, she hadn't said anything to him about it, but maintained an air of good-natured interest and eagerness to follow him on this adventure.

They had hardly spent a moment alone, but Osman thought she looked pretty and smart, and although she took care not to show it, she also had the capacity to take charge, and probably would, once she was settled. They'd be fixing up the police chief's living quarters, he thought, and she would supervise the decorating. He hoped she and Maryam would like each other.

His mother seemed relieved to have gotten him married to a woman of her choosing; she'd worried he'd be lassoed by a Kelantan girl over whom she would have little influence. This disaster had been averted, and she could rest easier when he returned to the east coast, knowing Azrina would make sure he returned to Perak. She'd done a fine job, if she said so herself.

Now that Osman was taken care of, it was time to turn her attentions to her daughters, who would probably be easier or, if not, at least closer.

Osman adjusted his carefully tied headcloth and turned to his new wife, who looked demurely down at her lap. 'Are you tired?' he whispered. 'I am.'

As soon as it was out, he regretted saying anything. What a fatuous comment! She would think him boring and stupid. However, she looked up at him from the corners of her eyes, and he was immediately enchanted. 'Me too! This is harder than it looks!' He leaned back in his chair, minimally, now content. This might work out well after all.

* * *

A familiar voice called from the bottom of the stairs, a voice nearly drowned out in the cacophony of excited, and aggressive, geese. Mamat looked up from the doves he was carefully feeding and saw Osman and what he surmised was his new wife.

'Welcome, welcome,' he cried as he pushed the geese out of the way and escorted them up the stairs. Most of the birds gathered around the bottom of the steps, eyeing the newcomers and honking to each other while flapping their wings, unhappy at being deprived of the chance to intimidate the intruders. Azrina watched the geese carefully from the safety of the porch and wondered how they'd get past them when they left.

Maryam came out of the house already bearing a tray of coffee, followed by Aliza bearing a platter of cookies. Both Maryam and

Aliza wore tight, concealing headscarves tied firmly around their heads to ensure there would be no slippage, making them look far more strictly religious than they actually were. Osman was shocked at how thin and pale both Maryam and Aliza looked. Maryam looked fatigued, and Aliza looked like a little girl again, not like the young woman she was rapidly becoming.

'I'm so glad to meet you,' Maryam said happily, reaching out both hands in a polite greeting. Aliza smiled and bent over her hand, then shyly retreated behind her mother, peeking out to evaluate Azrina. 'We've thought about you, wondering about the wedding,' Maryam told them.

'The *songket* was beautiful,' Azrina said, wanting it to be the first thing said lest it get lost in general conversation. 'I've never seen anything like it; everyone said so.' She smiled at Maryam. 'Thank you!'

Maryam blushed with pleasure. 'Oh, it was nothing. After all, this is where we make *songket*, so I thought Cik Osman should come back with some really excellent cloth.'

'I don't think we can even buy cloth like that in Perak,' Azrina continued. 'That kind of quality ...'

'That kind of cloth isn't usually sold elsewhere, just here,' Maryam said proudly, vaguely waving an arm to encompass the village of Kampong Penambang. 'It's woven right here, in this village.'

'*Alamak*!' Azrina bubbled. 'That's so exciting. I'm in the centre ...'

'Of the world of *songket*,' Maryam finished for her. She turned to Aliza and asked her to get Rubiah. With a shy smile,

Aliza hopped down the stairs and trotted off. The geese were silent, continuing to monitor the guests rather than bother Aliza, who had been known to kick them.

'Are you fixing up your quarters?' Maryam asked.

'Oh yes,' Azrina answered confidently. 'It was so plain! You know how things look when men live alone! Hardly any furniture, hardly any food. It looks like a prison.'

Maryam nodded, and Mamat put a consoling hand on Osman's shoulder and offered him a cigarette. He refused, as did Azrina, but Maryam took one gladly, and relaxed noticeably. 'I hope you'll like it here. I'm sure your being here will make *Cik* Osman like it more.'

Azrina giggled for a moment and nodded. Maryam thought she saw a flash of something more than a polite and shy new wife. Some strength, and a great deal of intelligence. Osman was lucky.

'How are you feeling, *Mak Cik*?' Maryam heard Osman saying and brought herself back to the conversation.

'Oh, a little better.' She wasn't sure if that was true, but it was the best answer she could give.

'Has the ceremony already ...?'

'No, in two days.' She sighed. 'I really hope it works.'

'Of course, it will,' Mamat insisted stoutly. 'You're going to feel like yourself again when it's over.'

'The ceremony?' Azrina interjected.

'A curing ceremony,' Osman explained. 'A *main puteri*.'

Azrina nodded but didn't really know what that was. They were rarely, if ever, performed in Perak.

'Should I be there, *Mak Cik*?'

Maryam wasn't sure how to answer. 'I guess so,' she said doubtfully.

'Well, not if it's private.'

'It isn't,' said Mamat. 'You should come. You never know what might come out.'

'What do you mean?' Maryam was suddenly frightened. 'What would come out?'

'Nothing should,' he soothed her. 'It's just a figure of speech.'

Maryam didn't believe him, but wasn't going to argue in front of Osman's new wife. So she smiled instead, and gestured towards the cakes, urging them to eat. 'Ah, here's *Mak Cik* Rubiah,' she announced, watching her cross the yard with Aliza. 'She can explain all about the cakes. She made them all!'

Maryam wasn't sure whether she hoped she would fall into trance at the *main puteri*, to get the most out of the experience, or hoped she would not, to avoid making a fool of herself. She feared it would be impossible to do both, and she dreaded an inconclusive and ineffectual ceremony leaving her in the same pain and unhappiness she now felt. But she also feared a rousing success which would have her friends and family talking forever about how hilarious she was, thinking she was a princess at her age. Either way, she would lose.

She prepared her house for the ceremony, sweeping and resweeping the yard until it was a clean and smooth surface on which *Pak* Nik Lah (or maybe both of them) could dance. She shuddered. *Please don't let me embarrass myself,* she prayed.

The evening of the ceremony arrived. *Pak* Nik Lah and his musicians were setting up in the yard, while neighbourhood children crouched just outside the hard ground. *Pak* Nik Lah was dressed in a plain sarong, tied up into the waist so that modesty would not be offended no matter how he moved.

Another sarong was rolled lengthwise and tied around the middle of his chest to provide a handle for his helper should he need to get him under control while he was in trance. The helper, called a *tok mindok*, would question him while in trance, speaking to the spirits through *Pak* Nik Lah, and keep the audience entertained with comedy before serious action got underway.

The *bomoh* was burning incense in a small brazier, sitting quietly before it, murmuring prayers and incantations to ready both himself and the place.

Small bowls of popped rice, flowers, water and coins were arranged around it and were thrown around the yard as offerings for the spirits to come. Coffee, cigarettes and snacks were put out for the troupe. They would be playing most of the night, and neighbours would continuously replenish their supplies in order keep up their strength.

Maryam, watching from a window, felt the preliminaries were going on forever, though the process was actually going much more quickly than she imagined. At last, *Pak* Nik Lah bent over the incense and cupped the smoke in his hands, then rubbing them up and down on his face. His incantations became slightly louder, and he rocked back and forth as he chanted. He was beginning his trance.

Maryam and her family sat along the edge of the area where

the dancing would take place. Everyone tried to sit as close to her as possible, to hold her hand or arm, to show their support and devotion. Mamat sat to one side, urging her to relax and lean back against him, while Malek sat on the other side, holding Aliza in front of him while Malek's wife, Zahara, held her hand.

All Maryam's friends from the village, and some from the market, were there, as were all her family and in-laws. Osman and Azrina were sitting farther away, among the neighbours. Osman watched anxiously, constantly looking around to see if anyone looked suspicious.

At this point in the ceremony, the crowd was light-hearted and eager. Nothing threatening, or frightening, had been unleashed, and most of the comedy routines were now being enacted. A few entrepreneurs set up small rickety stalls on the dirt path near the house, where coffee was being served, cigarettes shared, and bags of snacks sold out of large plastic buckets. It was a party.

People stopped to say hello to Maryam and Aliza, wish them luck, express their support. Unlike some *main puteri*, where the patients were ill, near to unconscious even, Maryam and Aliza, though thinner and paler than usual, were alert and even excited. In fact, they presided as hostesses at a celebration. They were, therefore, much more fun to talk to.

The music started, still soft and led by the *rebab,* a fiddle-like instrument played by the *tok mindok*, backed up with drums and gongs. The tunes, droning and repetitive, were trance-inducing on their own. *Pak* Nik Lah sat facing his helper and interlocutor, his eyes closed, introducing himself as a variety of *jinn* which then engaged in repartee.The festive air continued, the jokes were funny and based upon Kampong Penambang village gossip (of which, *Pak* Nik Lah had gotten an earful) and Maryam found her anxiety abating as time passed and no ridiculous antics were required of her.

Imperceptibly now, the atmosphere started to change. The music began to speed up, and the comedy was no longer as uproarious. *Pak* Nik Lah took longer to answer than he had before, and the questions put to him became more serious. The incense now seemed thicker to Maryam, and Aliza's eyes had trouble staying opened.

Pak Nik Lah now rose from sitting to adopt a dancer's pose: down on one knee, his hands curled back and held in front of him.

'Who are you?' demanded the helper, and when *Pak* Nik Lah remained silent, the question was repeated more loudly. Suddenly, *Pak* Nik Lah was on his feet, dancing with a martial attitude, announcing his name as a spirit who had been spurned, ignored, and therefore had invaded Maryam in order to get the attention he deserved.

He danced around the yard, then danced for a long time in front of Maryam, who began to feel light-headed and sleepy. She watched the *bomoh*, and then her eyes closed and she was no longer conscious.

The *tok mindok* kept pressing *Pak* Nik Lah, demanding the spirit tell them what he wanted, and what would make him leave Maryam and Aliza alone, allowing them to return to the health and energy they'd enjoyed before they were afflicted. There was only silence, and the audience leaned in closer, to hear what this troublesome spirit might demand: scarves or prayers or offerings.

With a sudden roar, *Pak* Nik Lah leaped back, higher than a man his size had any right to leap, and spoke furiously to his helper. He was the *pelesit*, he announced, kept in a bottle (as most *pelesit* were) on a ship, on the sea. A collective gasp arouse from the crowd. This was Murad's *pelsesit*, surely!

He needed feeding, he needed attention, he needed offerings. He'd worked hard for his human owners, and they had not given him what he deserved. (Now *Pak* Nik Lah's face was fearsome, and some of the smaller children watching began to cry as they scrambled towards their parents' laps.) He would desert them! Let them see how they fared without his help.

Mamat and Malek exchanged nervous looks. This looked more serious than they had expected. Malek was thankful Aliza was asleep, or entranced, so she wouldn't receive a further shock. Yi was frightened, but fascinated too, and sat behind his father looking over his shoulder, ready to duck if *Pak* Nik Lah so much as looked his way.

There were frissons of fear running through the crowd. No one expected a spirit they actually recognized. It was too close to home, though the owner's name was never mentioned.

Maryam suddenly rose in one swift motion and assumed a warrior's pose. Mamat sat with open mouth; where had she learned that? She spoke in a loud, clear voice to the pelesit, ordering it to leave her. She danced silat with *Pak* Nik Lah, a martial arts dance, lunging and dancing back, charging, but never being touched.

She spun on one foot, ending in a high kick which missed

the *bomoh* by millimetres. And behind her now, close, a faithful retainer, was Aliza, dancing like a sprite: so light, so graceful she hardly seemed human.

The *pelesit* fell back, guided by the *tok mindok*, now crying for mercy, if Maryam would just do him the favour of some offerings – some flowers, a few coins. He promised to leave them, to leave, in fact, his life of bad deeds and service of selfishness if Maryam would but grant him that.

As gracious in victory as she was fearless in battle, she agreed. She danced once around the circle, followed always by Aliza, who seemed to be floating on the air itself and then sat in front of Mamat before falling back, boneless. Malek caught Aliza in mid-fall, and gathered her up into his arms, inexplicably finding himself in tears.

Everyone agreed it was the best *main puteri* they had ever seen.

Chapter XXII

The family gathered back at the house. *Pak* Nik Lah came by to see how his patients were doing – they were both sound asleep. 'That's as it should be,' he said approvingly. 'That means it's working.'

Pak Nik Lah himself looked as though he could use some sleep. 'It's tiring,' he admitted, 'but if it works, then it's all worth it.'

Rubiah served him coffee and pressed large platters of cakes on his troupe, now packing up outside. They took their time getting their things together, pausing to eat, drink and smoke, speaking softly so as not to disturb those around them who might be trying to sleep.

Maryam and Aliza were put to sleep together in the children's bedroom, and Mamat turned off the lights and lay down in his own bed, watching the window. It had been an amazing ceremony. He'd seen plenty of *main puteri* in his time, but this was the first time his own immediate family had been involved, and it was an emotional upheaval.

He never expected to be as moved as he was, watching

Maryam and Aliza entranced: so brave, so lovely, so graceful. He'd been near to or in tears since Maryam first stood up. He thought he understood now why it was so often successful – the intensity of the trance, the immediacy of the spirits.

(And until then, Mamat wasn't even sure he really believed in spirits, and didn't expect to. But this ceremony had wrenched him out of his everyday existence and into another plane.)

In addition, the anxiety of hoping for a cure, all these things seemed to change the world he lived in. He'd expected a play, to be entertained, maybe be a little frightened. He hadn't expected to feel transported. But now he felt like a different person.

He thought he would fall into sleep immediately, but his mind wouldn't stop racing, so he lay there – alert, awake, considering the nature of the world and of spirits. He heard the noises of the *kampong* at night: the rustle of the doves in their cages on the porch, the settling of the geese in their baskets in the back, crickets and frogs.

It was soothing, after the noise and the crowd of the ceremony. The aftermath seemed so calm, so dark. A slight breeze rustled the palm fronds not far from the house; he could hear Yi turn in his sleep. And then ...

He wasn't sure he actually heard anything; had he imagined it? The softest possible footfall. He looked out the window, making no noise, but no shadows moved. He listened again, but the quiet was unbroken.

He was unable to relax now and told himself his imagination would not slow down. He eased himself up so he was sitting up in bed, leaning his back against the wall. He didn't want to get too close to the window, lest he be seen. His ears seemed preternaturally alert now, as though he could identify each individual cricket if he wanted to.

He thought he heard it again, and froze in place. Now the shadows seemed to move; was it the breeze moving the trees? He held his breath, and hoped Malek was awake as well, guarding Maryam and Aliza as they had agreed.

He didn't move his eyes from the window. It seemed an eternity in which nothing moved, no new noises presented themselves. And then, when he had almost convinced himself it was an overactive imagination, he saw a hand slowly come up onto the sill and stay there. And then the other hand. Mamat dared not even breathe. The fingers tightened on the sill, and a head and shoulders appeared, just leaning into the room.

Mamat propelled himself forward and grabbed the head, pulling the body into the room, roaring with rage, calling out to Malek and Daud and Osman, waiting silently in the living room, just inside the door. All the men crashed into the room, there was confused shouting. And then the lights turned on.

Kamal was splayed out on a bed, pinned down by Mamat at his head and Daud at his feet, and Osman already handcuffing him to the bed. All of them were breathing heavily, red in the face, and very angry.

'Well,' Osman demanded. 'Explain what you're doing here.'

Kamal looked around wildly, but said nothing. The veins in his neck pulsing, Osman pulled his arm roughly and demanded once more, 'Talk to me! What do you think you're doing?'

Yi's voice came to them from under the window. '*Ayah*! Look at this!'

Four of them leaned out to see Yi holding up a tall but thin wooden box placed under the window. 'He must have been standing on this,' said Yi proudly.

'Great work!' Osman smiled. 'He's a smart kid,' he said to Mamat as he turned to go out and gather his evidence.

'He gets it from his mother,' Mamat replied, taking a cigarette from the pack Daud passed around. They all relaxed now, congratulating each other while shooting dirty looks at Kamal, who sat morosely next to the bed rattling his handcuffs. Malek kicked his foot out of the way, looked at him insolently and muttered 'sorry' in the most unapologetic way possible.

Kamal appeared to be in for a very long night. Minutes later, they heard the sound of a police car arriving in Kampong Penambang, and Osman coming noisily up the stairs.

'Look what I found!' he announced, pushing a dishevelled Hamidah into the room in front of him. 'She was hiding in the bushes,' he said disgustedly. 'Can you imagine? A woman her age?'

Her hair was matted in disarray, her face smudged with dirt, her hands filthy and her sarong black at the knees. And she was smiling – a horrible, lopsided smile which made her look like a ghoul.

Rubiah and her husband Dollah were over soon after, as dawn began to break and the first call to prayer broke the sleeping silence. She brought a full breakfast for everyone, and began making coffee and reheating the mound of curry puffs she'd brought as well, should anyone appear to be faint. The night's heroics made everyone hungry and elated, and when Maryam and Aliza woke and emerged, they were greeted with congratulations and cheers. Both were smiling broadly.

'How are you feeling, *sayang*?' asked Mamat.

She beamed at him. 'I wouldn't have believed it. I didn't think it would happen. I feel so much better! Like another person!' She looked at Aliza, who smiled back, more shyly than her mother.

'I think I'm better,' she said, running her hand over the stubble on her head. 'And I think my hair is longer.'

'I think so, too,' Yi assured her. 'I can definitely see it.'

'When this scar fades,' Maryam announced, as Malek winced – he couldn't bear hearing about the *enam sembilan* mark on her forehead – 'I'll be as good as new. No one will ever know this happened. Even me!'

Rubiah threw her arms around Maryam, laughing and crying at the same time. 'I'm so happy,' she whispered to her. 'I was so afraid.'

'So was I,' Maryam admitted. 'But I feel like it's behind me now, or will be soon. I'm going to be fine.'

They both turned to Aliza to admire her. 'Do you remember any of it?'

'Not really,' Aliza confessed. 'Did I dance?'

'Did you dance?' her father asked, giddy with relief. 'I've never seen anyone dance so beautifully. Like an angel, like a *bidadari*! It was amazing.'

Malek nodded enthusiastically. 'Your feet hardly touched the ground!' he assured her. 'It was something to see!'

'You were lovely!' Rubiah added, caressing her head for a moment. She then handed her a plate piled with her favourite cakes, and *nasi kerabu* wrapped in a banana leaf. This latter was a hearty Kelantan breakfast of blue rice cooked in coconut milk, topped with fish and vegetables and egg.

'Now, you'd better eat and get all your strength back!' Rubiah was a great believer in the restorative powers of cakes, which she considered a miracle food.

'Do you remember anything?' Mamat asked Maryam.

She shook her head. 'Not really. Not after I saw *Pak* Nik Lah dancing in front of me.'

'Well, you danced silat, you know,' Mamat told her. 'Like a real warrior. I don't know where you learned it.'

'Silat?' Maryam considered this. 'I don't know anything about silat.'

'You don't think you do, but believe me, you can do it! I was never so surprised.'

Surprise filled her face, as she applied herself to curry puffs and coffee. 'It gives you quite an appetite,' she explained. 'I'm starved.'

Rubiah looked beneficently on, wholeheartedly approving of this show of hunger. It was, in her eyes, the best possible outcome.

Chapter XXIII

Kamal and his mother were at the police station, waiting to be questioned. There was no celebratory breakfast for them – no cakes, no coffee. No one offered them anything, even though Kamal had asked.

'Later,' Rahman told him briefly, leaving them both sitting in the large office, cuffed to chairs. 'Wait for Police Chief Osman,' he said formally, and then the whole station set about ignoring them completely, save for ordering them to be quiet if either of them said anything.

Without a hint of flagging, Hamidah kept her smile, though for everyone else, it was difficult to look at without shuddering.

Osman came back, flushed with victory and two full helpings of *nasi kerabu*, in addition to countless cakes. He felt heavier than usual, a feeling he often found after being subjected to Rubiah's ministrations. This time, however, going to sleep in his chair was not an option. He definitely wanted to hear the suspects' story. It promised to be interesting, at least.

They were brought into the office he thought of as his interrogation room, furnished only with a long wooden table and some serviceable chairs. There were no pictures and no decoration – in other words, nothing to distract a suspect from dispensing the truth.

Osman longed to order Hamidah to stop smiling: it unnerved him, but he thought telling her anything would probably have no effect. He asked Kamal instead. 'Please ask your mother to stop grinning at me. I can't look at it any longer.'

Kamal looked over at his mother, who appeared not to have heard. '*Mak*,' he said loudly, 'He wants you to stop smiling.'

Hamidah looked surprised. 'Why?'

'He doesn't like it.'

She nodded and tried to tone it down. Though as soon as she became straight-faced, the full-force smile broke through again, as though she was privy to a private joke she could not get over. Osman watched this happen twice, then sighed and turned away. He looked at Rahman, sitting quietly in the corner, who shrugged and raised his eyebrows.

Indeed. Questioning a madwoman did not seem the best use of time, but what if she was only faking madness in order to get away with some awful crimes? The fury he felt when he had first seen Kamal dragged in through the window had abated but not disappeared, and he felt his patience with this pair running short. He fully understood the urge of some of his colleagues to beat the truth out of recalcitrant perpetrators – but would not succumb to it himself.

'Tell me, Kamal,' he began conversationally, 'what were you doing in Kampong Penambang last night?'

The young suspect fidgeted, but said nothing.

'You're wasting my time,' Osman told him bluntly. 'If you'd prefer to sit in jail for a few days before you decide to tell me, that's fine with me. I don't mind going home, I've been up all night.'

He waited. Kamal stared at the floor.

'Good. Your choice.' He got up and walked into the main room. 'Go ahead, put both of them in the cells. I'm going home.' Kamal looked at him with something approaching horror, but Osman steeled himself not to look back, and did, in fact, head home. Where Azrina was very happy to see him.

'What happened? Alamak! You look so tired!'

'I am.' But it was a real pleasure to have someone at home to talk to about it. He smiled at her. 'I'm glad you're here.'

'Do you want to – I mean, can you, anyway – tell me anything?'

He nodded. 'Some. Do you really want to hear?'

She nodded eagerly. (She also was a devotee of crime novels, which had made the prospect of Osman as a husband so interesting.) The whole caper, as she thought of it, became all the more real when Osman told her he was staying at Maryam's, and a group of them would await developments. He called another officer to see her home safely, and she was thrilled at the thought her husband was lying in ambush.

Was this a typical Kelantan evening, she wondered: *spirit possession followed by criminal activity?* Indeed, Kota Bharu was more exotic than she had hoped. Nothing like this ever happened to her in Perak.

Osman told her what had happened, including how Kamal had

been handcuffed to the bed. She was wide-eyed with admiration, a reaction Osman had not seen very often, especially in Kelantan. He told her about finding Hamidah, looking as though she had just crawled through the dirt, with that weird smile on her face, very much like an evil spirit herself. 'They're both in jail right now, where they'll stay until they decide to talk. I think she's not well,' he said expansively. 'She looks crazy. She acts crazy. But I still don't know if she really is; it could be a game with her, a way of doing things and not being held responsible for it.'

To his own ears, he sounded immensely more mature and professional than he had before. And if it was so easy to do here – why did he have so much trouble doing it when any of the Kelantan women were around? With them, he could barely open his mouth. Perhaps, he decided, he should practice on them and see if they noticed.

He remembered with a sinking heart the looks they gave him when he tried to hold forth, and he quailed. Looking over at Azrina, however, with her hands over her mouth in awe, he gained confidence again, and told her about it all over again.

Aziz heard the news of Kamal's attempted entry and subsequent arrest with unspoken relief. Since Rahim and Zaiton's return home from their Sungei Golok escapade, he had not brought up the search for Jamillah's murderer, preferring to let it lie. He wanted no more drama in his life, and feared if he asked too many questions, he could stumble upon answers he didn't want to hear; the safest course, then, was to steer clear of the whole subject, a project in which the young couple seemed only too eager to assist.

He had never been able to fathom the attack on Maryam, and why Zaiton was so frightened that it was Rahim who did it. She could cry and claim confusion and wring her hands all she wanted, but her father considered her first comments that evening the most truthful, and in those it was clear to him she believed Rahim had done it and, indeed, been caught.

Probably then, there had been a plan between the two, and she realized too late she'd implicated Rahim. Aziz was too tired to pursue it, and far too tired to actually hear the truth. He already knew it; he hoped the police didn't. It was a shame Maryam was hurt, and Aliza, too, but implicating Rahim wouldn't help them though it would hurt Zaiton and the baby.

Maybe these things were now best left alone, and that included Jamillah's death. Though if he were to confide this to anyone, they might easily misunderstand.

Kamal trying to leap into Maryam's house through the bedroom window did not surprise him. He had never really liked the boy, whom he considered as cold and conceited as his father, and his inheritance of the boat along with all the capital which rightly belonged to Aziz, merely sealed it. He could not for a moment entertain the thought that Kamal knew nothing about the transfer, or hadn't rubbed his hands in delight (literally or metaphorically, it made no difference) upon learning of that deal which would benefit him as it would diminish others. Father or son would both be willing to climb into windows and smother innocent women in their sleep. And if they were aided by a *pelesit*, it was all the more likely.

He'd never seen a known spirit called by name, a spirit

he'd actually heard about, as he had at Maryam's *main puteri*; though admittedly, he was no expert. But most spectators took it as absolute validation of the spirit's existence – they'd heard it actually speak and reveal itself as Murad's very own familiar.

Though unmentioned and unnoticed at the time, rumours now began circulating of a large, malignant grasshopper, the embodiment of the pelesit itself, seen in the area of Maryam's house after the ceremony.

Some more creative minds described a grasshopper as big as a child, on which Kamal stood when trying to get into Maryam's house. Others claimed that Kamal himself turned into such a creature when he was apprehended. That would have been something to see, Aziz thought, and certainly would have warranted Mamat and the others running screaming from the house.

Still, he expected the stories to get wilder as they travelled. Soon it would be said the whole *kampong* turned into grasshoppers and flew off into the jungle.

He wished someone would ask him about it; almost nothing would give him more pleasure than to be able to seal the fate of Murad's family. He didn't know whether Hamidah had been so corrupted by that family she'd married into that she now cared for their evil spirits and assisted in their attacks; he'd like to think she hadn't.

He remembered Hamidah fondly and had a childish crush on her before either of them had seriously considered marriage. Although right now he was content, it was possible that one day he'd want to marry again for the companionship, and Hamidah might have made his short list. Except, of course, that she was already married and people said she was mad.

He considered the possibility that divorcing Murad might cure the madness – who wouldn't be crazy if they had to live with that bitter old man and his trolls? People said she looked like a vampire, like a corpse risen from the grave. The gossip in the *kampong* was that she was now filthy and unkempt, with a mad, unnerving smile and matted hair. No one actually said she was wearing a shroud like a *langsuir,* a vampire-like female spirit which preyed on pregnant women, but the implication was clear.

He sighed with regret that such a pretty and light-hearted girl should become an old woman like this. *Untong sabat timbul, untong batu tenggelam:* the fate of the husk is to float, the fate of the stone is to sink. To elude your fate was impossible. That was true for everyone, but Hamidah's was particularly harsh.

* * *

Murad arrived at the police station spoiling for a fight, and Osman was not in a conciliatory frame of mind. *Anjing galak, babi pun berani:* the dogs are ready and the wild boar is brave. No one would back down. Osman looked up from his desk to see Murad come in, dressed all in white: white sarong, white *baju melayu*, white cap. The choice of colour alone annoyed him.

'Can I help you, *Pak Cik* Murad?' he asked politely.

'I hear you have my wife and son in jail!' he shouted at Osman accusingly. 'I want them out!'

'I'm afraid that's impossible,' Osman told him, looking grave but feeling gleeful in delivering bad news. This family brought out the worst in everyone. 'They were caught in the act of breaking into someone's house.'

'Maryam's,' Murad sneered, as though that would explain it all.

'Yes.'

'Well, don't you think when you interfere in people's affairs like she does, it's more likely things like this will happen? She'll have to take some responsibility for what happens to her.'

'She was helping the police,' Osman replied icily. 'I don't take that as an invitation to break in and attack her. I'm sorry, your wife and son are being charged and are not free to go.'

Murad looked down his nose at Osman, his rising anger showing in his eyes. 'How dare you hold them. I want them at home.'

'It doesn't matter,' Osman answered. 'Now, if you will excuse me …'

Murad tried another tack. 'My wife is not well.'

'*Pak Cik* Murad,' he said with exaggerated patience, 'she is under arrest. She will not be let go because she isn't well, she was well enough to help your son break into a house. Now, good evening.'

In high dudgeon, Murad stalked out of the office, straight to Osman's residence on the grounds of the station, calmly picked up a rock and heaved it through a window. Osman thought he heard the tinkle of glass, but ignored it, still seething from his discussion with the bumptious Murad. He had a good mind to arrest him for killing Jamillah right now, just to show him he could.

Minutes later, Azrina flew into the station, 'Someone broke one of our windows!'

'What?'

'Yes, in the kitchen. I saw him: a tall, older man wearing all white and the meanest expression I ever saw.'

Osman was already headed for the door. 'Did he see you, too?'

'I don't know. He didn't throw it at me, if that's what you mean. But it was definitely deliberate. Who is he?'

'Murad.'

'That's the one,' she said with interest. *Imagine! A suspect right here!*

'Rahman, take two other men with you and bring him in. He can't just throw rocks at us and think he'll go home and relax! Go!'

Rahman moved right away to get him; he reckoned he could head him off on the street. He couldn't have gone far.

Osman went into his house with Azrina, examining the broken glass on the floor and the not particularly big rock lying in the midst of it. Sitting now on the rock, seeming to look at him, was a grasshopper.

Chapter XXIV

Maryam was now not only feeling better, she felt more than recovered. She felt bouncy. She didn't know whether to credit the *main puteri* alone, or the enforced rest she'd had before it. (Rubiah believed it was both; without the *main puteri* hanging over her, Maryam would never have allowed either herself to rest or anyone else to suggest it.)

The mark still remained, but it was fading, albeit slowly; besides, Maryam was becoming used to the headscarf. She estimated another month before Aliza's hair would just look very short, and she too could leave the scarf at home.

She was ready to take the reins again on the investigation, which she regarded as becalmed without her leadership. Osman was summoned to her house for a general discussion, during which he offered a *précis* of what had gone on, and what had not. There appeared little progress in actually finding who killed Jamillah and far too much talk about grasshoppers, which had no bearing on the case.

'We aren't here to catch a *pelesit*,' she reminded him curtly, and could not resist adding, 'even if your wife would really enjoy it.'

Osman looked hurt, but didn't argue. Maryam elaborated. 'I know she's really interested in the case, I could see it when she visited, and that's wonderful. She's your wife, she should be. But let's not concentrate on all the ...' she thought for a minute, then waved a dismissive hand, 'exotic Kelantan ... spirits and such. There seem to be plenty of flesh and blood suspects who could have done it without getting into *jinn*.'

She looked at him meaningfully, expecting agreement, which she received. She scratched her scarf around her mark. 'It's itchy,' she told him. 'I can't wait till it's healed.'

She then returned to the matter of apprehending the killer. 'Rubiah thinks it's Murad, but that's because she doesn't like him.'

'I don't like him either,' Osman said. 'I don't like the whole family, and I'd be very happy to throw all of them in jail. But we've got to prove something first.'

'I hate to think Rahim ...'

'We've left him alone ...'

'No more,' Maryam told him decisively. 'It's time to wrap this up.'

Which led directly to Rahim sitting in Osman's office, at the large, scraped table on a chair with one leg slightly shorter than the rest, facing Maryam directly. Osman, as was often his habit, sat off to the side, taking notes and occasionally interjecting when he felt strongly about a comment.

'Rahim,' Maryam began mournfully, 'When I first met you, I thought you were such a nice boy. A man, I mean. Hard-working, polite, honest. Both *Mak Cik* Rubiah and I talked about how pleased *Mak Cik* Jamillah must have been to see her daughter with such a man.'

Without any money, she forbore to add, but she believed Jamillah would have gotten past that, had she lived. All market women knew that hard work formed the basis of good business. Rahim hung his head and looked embarrassed and uncomfortable. Well, that was a sign of decent character, anyway.

'And then you ran off to get married. Marriage is a good thing, and given what you did, it was the only thing. I wished you two hadn't done it, it's wrong, and I don't defend it, but having done it, you did what you had to. *Mak Cik* Jamillah would have agreed, I'm sure.

'But when Zaiton grabbed Aliza, and hurt her like she did,' both Rahim and Osman winced just thinking about it, 'that changes everything. Now Zaiton cried and looked confused and the men in the *kampong* and the police, they didn't want to press it. There was enough going on, with two serious head wounds.'

She looked hard at him, but he wouldn't meet her eyes.

'But Ashikin thought – and you know, I listen to her, because she's smart.' Osman could not have agreed more heartily, but would himself have added 'intimidating'. 'Zaiton believed you'd attacked me and was trying to draw attention away from you.' She flicked the ashes of her cigarette into a battered ashtray, and Osman silently leaned over to offer her another. Rahim also took one.

'What do you think of what I've said?'

'You won't believe me now.'

'Maybe not. But you really must try. Right, *Cik* Osman?'

Osman nodded and looked official.

Rahim sighed. 'I was going over to see you, *Mak Cik*. Not to hit you over the head, why would I do that? And where would I have gotten an *enam sembilan*? I wanted to talk to you and tell you what was happening with us, that we were going to Sungei Golok and why, so you wouldn't think we were two suspects running away. Though why you would suspect anyone of killing their own parents ...' No one spoke.

'So I was coming to see you. And as I was coming into the *kampong*, I heard all the commotion and realized you'd been hurt. I decided not to continue, because if I came there to help, everyone would ask what I was doing there, and our secret would have come out, and everyone would know.'

'Everyone knows now,' Maryam pointed out to him.

He nodded sadly. 'I was hoping to do it quietly, but then, after what happened with Zaiton – and *Mak Cik*, I'm very sorry it did – she couldn't tell her father, so she just left, and then he went to the police, of course, and then ... well, you know. But it wasn't because I didn't want to help you. There were so many people around I knew you'd be cared for, and I still thought, like I said, we could keep it quiet and no one would know.

'I look back now and think how stupid I was, believing that no one would find out. And if I had come forward, you wouldn't be asking me this.'

'Probably not,' Maryam agreed.

'After the *main puteri*, Zaiton went to speak to her mother, to ask her when we could get married. I was in the house, but not in the room with them. I couldn't hear them, but I could see *Mak*

Cik Jamillah was tired, and I don't think she wanted to discuss it then. I tried to tell Zaiton that earlier; a couple of days more wouldn't make any difference. But she can be stubborn.' Maryam silently agreed.

'She went right into the bedroom with her mother, saying she was going to help her into bed, but I know she wanted to talk about it. Then she came out a few minutes later and said her mother was sleeping, which the *bomoh* told us would happen.' Maryam knew all about that. 'And then I went home.'

'So *Mak Cik* Jamillah didn't come out of the bedroom again after Zaiton put her to sleep.'

'No, she was asleep. Well, she didn't come out while I was there anyway. Maybe she did after I left? But Zaiton said she was asleep.'

'So Zaiton would have been the last to see her.'

'Except for her father. I mean, he was sleeping right next to her.'

'True.'

Rahim looked at her with horror. 'You don't mean you're thinking ...? That wouldn't be possible. No.' He looked from one to the other.

'We're thinking everything, Rahim,' she said tiredly. 'We're keeping an open mind.'

'That's it. You can go now,' Osman told him. 'But not to Thailand, you understand?' Rahim nodded glumly. 'Because if you try that again, I'll arrest you.'

He nodded again and shuffled out of the office. He looked broken.

Chapter XXV

Maryam, Rubiah and Osman sat on Aziz's porch drinking coffee, smoking cigarettes and eating Rubiah's cakes while an anxious Zaiton hovered nearby, offering more refreshments and looking to her father for help.

Maryam reflected it was actually quite pleasant sitting here, if you didn't remember why you came. It was late afternoon, so the air was cooler than it had been at noon, the cakes were excellent, the cigarettes were Osman's, and the coffee thick and sweet. Really, a Kelantan paradise; but then thinking about being here to question people ruined the atmosphere. She strove to enjoy her coffee and cigarette before settling down to business.

'How are you feeling?' she asked Zaiton.

'Oh fine,' she answered nervously, looking constantly toward her father as though he might know better how she felt.

'Not sick in the mornings?'

'Well, maybe sometimes.'

'Eat plain rice when you get up,' Rubiah advised. 'It'll settle your stomach.'

Zaiton nodded and fidgeted.

'*Pak Cik* Aziz,' Osman asked finally, 'would you mind if we spoke to Zaiton alone for a moment?'

With a long look at his daughter, who looked back imploringly, he turned and walked down the stairs. Rahman invited him for a coffee at a nearby stall, and they walked away together, with Aziz frequently looking back as if to send Zaiton moral support.

Rubiah was at her most maternal: understanding and sympathetic, yet allowing no nonsense. 'Now Zaiton, tell us what happened after the *main puteri*.'

'What do you mean?'

'Just what I said. After the ceremony, did your mother go to bed? She must have been tired.'

'I know I was,' Maryam chimed in.

'Yes, she was. I helped her to bed.'

'Did you discuss anything with her?'

'She was tired.'

'Did you talk about your wedding?'

'She was tired …'

'Zaiton,' Rubiah adjusted her glasses and looked down her nose at the girl. 'If you don't want to answer questions here …'

'We did … a little.'

'And?'

'She was very tired, like I told you. She just wanted to go to sleep. She said we could talk in the morning.'

'Why was that a problem?'

Zaiton commenced squirming, making Rubiah herself nervous. 'It was just that, you see …'

'Listen to me,' Maryam said softly, but with menace, 'I

think we've all had enough of your acting and crying and being confused. Now, you tell us what happened without any more fuss. And hurry up!'

Zaiton looked pleadingly at Osman, who sat stone-faced. He agreed she had been allowed to get away with this far too long. She deflated.

'It was just that I wanted to get it going! She'd put it off a couple of times because she was sick and she was waiting to have the *main puteri* finished first. She knew I had to do something soon! I didn't want to wait till morning, and then she'd say she had to have breakfast first, and then something else, and before you know it, even more time would have passed and then what? I told her, and she just lay down and fell asleep! Just like that.'

'Did you do anything to her?'

'Do anything?'

'To keep her awake?'

'No, why? There was no point. She was already asleep.'

'Are you sure you didn't shake her or anything?'

'Are you asking me if I killed my own mother?'

'I'm asking if you shook her.'

'No! She was asleep. She wasn't going to talk about anything.'

'Was the window opened in the bedroom?'

Zaiton thought about it. 'Yes, about halfway. The shutters were opened a little. She liked fresh air.'

Rubiah nodded. She did, too.

'And one more thing. Did your father go to sleep right away after that?'

'No, my relatives were all here, Zainab and her family. We

stayed up for a while, we were all so happy that she was cured. No one was in a hurry to go to sleep.'

Zaiton was dispatched to the kitchen when her father came back, and they reconvened on the porch. Again, coffee was served, cigarettes offered, cakes passed around. Maryam was putting her weight back on faster than she would have thought possible – but then, for the past weeks she'd been living on a cake-heavy diet.

'Is she alright?' Aziz asked about Zaiton.

'Of course, she is. Why wouldn't she be?'

'I'm just asking. I thought she looked upset.' He craned his neck as if trying to see through the wall of the house to the kitchen.

'Nothing to be upset about,' Maryam said briskly. '*Abang* Aziz, tell me, what happened after the *main puteri*?'

Aziz shrugged. 'We came back here, all the family. Jamillah was so tired, she was practically asleep standing up. Zaiton took her into the bedroom to put her to sleep.'

'Did they argue?'

'No, I didn't hear anything. She was asleep!'

'Alright. And then?'

He looked confused. 'Well, we talked for a while. Zainab was here with her family, and Jamillah's sisters, and my family. We just sat here and talked.'

'For how long?'

'Oh, at least two hours, I would think.'

'And you went to sleep after that?'

'Yes.'

'Next to Jamillah?'

'Where else?' He seemed mystified.

'And she seemed fine when you went to sleep.'

'She seemed asleep!' He began to look angry. 'Did I check her? No, she was asleep, turned away towards the window. And I went to sleep. And in the morning, I tried to wake her, and you know what happened then. You were here!'

'Yes,' Maryam said, absently. 'Did you notice anyone hanging around the house?'

Now he was angry. 'If I had, don't you think I would have said so already? Would I have kept quiet about it?' He glared at all of them. 'What a question!'

'I'm just asking, *Abang*,' she said mildly. 'Just trying to get all the facts together.'

'Well, now you have them.' Aziz stood up, ending the meeting. 'So you can do with them what you like.'

Chapter XXVI

'He thinks Zaiton killed her,' Maryam told Osman as they walked back to her house. 'That's why he's so angry.'

'Really? How could he live with her?'

Maryam shrugged. 'I'm just telling you that's what I see there. Rubiah?'

Rubiah was adjusting her headscarf and pushed her glasses farther up her nose. 'It's very sad,' she replied. 'It feels like that to me, too. He's lost his wife and doesn't want to lose his daughter and grandchild now. It's a terrible choice.'

Osman protested. 'But how can he protect a child who's killed her mother?'

'I didn't say she had,' Maryam told him, kicking away a goose who was following her and getting ready to start making noise. 'I just said Aziz thinks so, or is afraid so. That's why he isn't pushing anyone to hurry up the investigation.

'Zainab may agree, because no one's heard from her either, have they? You would think for something like this, the family wouldn't leave you alone about finding the killer. It's odd they're just sitting quietly.'

'No more coffee for me,' Osman said, as he held up a restraining hand. 'Please.'

'You aren't hungry?' Rubiah asked, unwilling to send him home without a meal.

'Oh no,' he assured her. 'We've been eating all day.'

'Maybe you have,' Rubiah chided him. 'We've been talking.'

He laughed, something he never would have done with either Maryam or Rubiah before, where he would only have felt rebuked and then apologized. But his confidence had grown since his marriage, and he no longer interpreted every comment as a reprimand – even if it was.

'Do you think we should talk to Zainab?'

Maryam thought about it. 'Of course. We should speak to the whole family.'

* * *

Zainab's story matched those of her sister and father. 'You had to clean up the whole mess with Zaiton, didn't you?' Maryam asked sympathetically. 'It must have been so hard on you, like taking over as the mother.'

Zainab agreed. 'I just don't know why Zaiton did what she did. Making me go all the way to Golok to find her, running away like that. At least everything worked out in the end. We had the *kenduri*, *Mak Cik*, and I think it went very well.'

'An excellent idea,' Maryam congratulated her. 'I think you handled it beautifully. No one could have done any better.'

'Thank you!' Zainab seemed pleased. 'I did try to get it all straightened out.'

'Tell me,' Maryam leaned forward confidentially, 'did you think Rahim had anything to do with the *enam sembilan*? I'm just asking your opinion. He says he was on his way here and then saw what happened and ran. I like him, you know. He's a nice boy.'

'We *thought* he was a nice boy,' Rubiah added.

'I don't know, *Mak Cik*. I know I should say "No, never!", and I'm not accusing anyone, but that whole situation was so tense and mixed up, I don't know what either of them were doing. I don't think they were thinking clearly either. I mean, now they're home and everything is quiet, and I don't doubt it will stay that way. Zaiton and I are going to take over my mother's stall in the market.'

'Congratulations! We'll be neighbours!'

Zainab smiled back at her. 'I know. Things have already settled down. It was a crazy time.'

Maryam and Rubiah smiled pleasantly and thanked her.

'She thinks it too,' Rubiah said as they left. 'She's telling us it won't happen again, so we should leave it alone.'

'I can understand why they wouldn't want to go through any more scandal. But a crime like that – it's unnatural! It makes me shiver.' She wrapped her arms around herself to demonstrate. 'If they all think Zaiton killed her mother, than it's most likely one of them who attacked me to make me stop investigating. But then, and this bothers me, what was Kamal doing climbing into my house?

Rubiah had no answer.

* * *

Osman could not understand Hamidah. Two female officers, assisted by Azrina, attempted to bathe her, which resulted in the three of them becoming soaked to the bone, while Hamidah's hair remained untouched and most of her dirt still in place.

'I don't know what's wrong with her!' Azrina exclaimed to Osman later. She fought like a tiger: *seperti polong kena sembur*, like a familiar spirit touched by water! She almost threw herself out of the room. And why? She wouldn't put on clean clothes or comb her hair.' Azrina gritted her teeth in frustration. 'Unbelievable. She really must be crazy, you know. What grown person would act that way? She's filthy!'

He watched as she stormed around the house shaking her head at the recalcitrance of the woman. He was completely content.

'Let's go to the night market,' he suggested. 'We can get some food there. Or eat by the river.' She smiled at him, excited now at the thought of exploring Kota Bharu after dark. 'Yes, I'll get my bag.' And she left him in the kitchen.

'Look at this,' she came back in, holding a small, shredded piece of yellow cloth with Thai writing on it. It had been balled up into the smallest size possible and was grubby with smeared black fingerprints.

'What do you think it is?' she asked him, trying to flatten it out so they could see what it said. Osman felt his back go cold. Azrina smoothed it out on the table; even out to its full length it was small, and he couldn't read Thai anyway. But there was no mistaking the small drawing of a demon face in the corner, slightly obscured by dirt but clear enough if you were looking hard. He put his hand on his forehead, and carefully removed her hand from it. 'Where did you get it?' he asked.

'I don't know.' She cocked her head to look at it from another angle. 'It isn't mine. Could Hamidah have stuck it into my clothes before? It looks like something she would have: dirty. Look at it.'

She looked up at him and her faced creased in concern. 'What is it?'

'I think it's a spell, a *jampi*. And it must be from her. No one else would have one so smudged.' He couldn't take his eyes off it. 'Let me take it, *sayang*. Don't even think about it.'

He took the offending object and tried to look insouciant, but it unnerved him. 'I don't want it in the house,' he said suddenly. 'Let's leave it in the office on our way out.'

He resolved to bring it to *Pak* Nik Lah first thing in the morning and find out what this family was trying to do to him. He kept a sharp eye out for grasshoppers, but saw none for the rest of the evening. Thankfully.

* * *

'At least it isn't poisonous,' Maryam told him. She didn't waste much time on the spell when Osman brought it to her. 'Heaven only knows what else she's got stuck into pockets and what-not. This is probably the cleanest thing on her.'

She kept her manner completely businesslike. 'What do these

little scribbles mean? It's *poison* you worry about. Besides,' she whipped a batik sarong open to show to a customer, 'that woman is crazy.'

Osman was a bit insulted that Maryam made such short shrift of this *jampi*. After all, hadn't she herself suffered under the curse of black magic?

'It was the poison,' she answered briefly. 'Not yellow cloth. Anyway, you should be finding out what that family is up to. I can't figure it out.'

Chapter XXVII

He strode into the holding cells in the police department – hardly a jail, just three rooms with bars. The air was heavy and hot: there was no air conditioning and only a small window in each cell, hardly sufficient for a breeze.

He went first to Kamal, sitting wretchedly on the hard bench, his head in his hands, looking as though he'd been sitting in that posture for years. He leaned in through the bars, his habitual expression of disapproval and distain unchanged, even seeing his only child in such straits. Kamal lifted his head to look at him without any warmth.

'What is it?'

'Is that how you talk to me?' his father asked. If he was surprised at the lack of deference he'd come to expect from his son, his face didn't reveal it.

Kamal was tired. 'What did you come here for, *Ayah*?'

'To see how you were.'

'How did you think I would be?'

'Stop talking in riddles,' he answered. Behind him, two policemen entered and unlocked the remaining empty cell. They ushered him into it with little ceremony, ran their eyes along the three sets of bars and left.

'You're in jail?' Kamal asked, shocked.

His father sniffed. 'I came to demand they release you, and they refused.'

'So?' asked Hamidah from the cell next to him.

'You're filthy!' he informed her.

'I know. Why are you here?'

'I threw a rock through the window there.' He waved towards Osman's house.

She nodded sagely. 'And left a grasshopper?'

'Don't talk about it,' he hissed at her. 'Not in here.'

'It's just a grasshopper.'

He glared at her, though it was difficult in side-by-side cells. She laughed at him, which clearly goaded him. 'You still think you're commanding the forces of evil?'

'You've fed it yourself. Be quiet.'

The tops of the walls were wire mesh, a half-hearted attempt to encourage the movement of air. It was a failure, but it allowed some contact among the cells, if indeed such contact was welcomed. Hamidah stepped onto her bench, which brought her to the mesh if she stood on tiptoe. She looked down into her husband's cell and smiled.

'It's nice to see you here, all locked up like this. Like a rooster in a cage: *bagai se ekur burong, mata lepas, badan terkurong.* Your eyes are free, but your body confined.'

'Get down from there.' He looked up at her disgustedly. 'Kamal, tell your mother to climb down off that bench. I can't bear to look at her.'

'Am I frightening you? How could that be?'

'Not you, Midah. Just the way you look – like a vampire with that hair. And a dirty face. Is this what you're really like?'

'Oh yes,' she agreed amiably. 'This is the real me, feeding spirits with blood, drinking it myself. It's what you made me. You should be proud to see it.'

He leaned back against the wall and closed his eyes. 'I don't know how I stayed married to you for so long.'

'I wonder the same thing; about myself, I mean.'

'Stop it!' Kamal ordered them. 'Just be quiet.'

'Kamal, it's just a conversation. Just family time here. This is where your father's taken us.'

'Be quiet, *Mak*.'

She leaned her elbows on the top of the wall. 'No more. Not for anyone.' She looked down at Murad. 'Where is your pelesit now? Is it coming to get us all out of here? I'm looking around and I don't see anything.'

'Be quiet,' Murad muttered again. 'Let me relax.'

'You can relax when you're dead,' she said with sudden vehemence. 'Just like you killed Jamillah.'

'Me?' He seemed honestly surprised. 'I didn't kill anyone.'

'I know you did. And I'm telling them! You think Kamal and I will sit still and be accused of your crimes? No more. You can suffer on your own.'

'Tell them what? There's nothing to tell.'

'They think you did it anyway, because no one can stand you. When I tell them, they'll be delighted to hear it. You're their favourite suspect. Maybe they'll hang you!'

'*Mak*, stop it!'

'Won't Noriah be crushed,' she taunted him. 'She might never recover!'

Murad was now furious. He pulled his bench over to the wall under the mesh, and climbed up on it. The veins in his neck were pulsing, his face was red, his teeth gritted.

'Leave Noriah out of this. This is just you being ... vindictive. I always told you, Midah, you can't always chase revenge.'

'You tell me that! You!'

They stood face to face through the wire, Murad's revulsion clear on his face, Hamidah spitting fury. He poked his finger into her face. 'I'm telling you to stop. You're a spectacle.'

She laughed at him, loud and long. 'I'm free of you now. You'll never get out of jail.'

In a rage, he grabbed her hair, and she howled with pain.

'Now listen! I divorce you! I divorce you! I divorce you! Kamal, do you hear it? Three *talak*! I never want to hear anything more from you.'

He yanked her hard by her hair, pounding her head onto the top of the wall. She squirmed around, trying to get free, but succeeded only in twisting his hand deeper into her hair so that he couldn't get loose.

Rahman and another officer came into the jail, drawn by Hamidah's screams, paralyzed by the tableau before them. They could hardly credit what they saw.

With a piercing scream, Hamidah desperately fought free a wicked-looking small dagger folded into her sarong, reached around and stabbed Murad in the neck. He could not jump away with his hand securely tangled in her hair, so she stabbed him again, blood now covering them both from the shoulders up.

He coughed and pulled his head back, but she kept the knife buried, and with a deft movement, slit his throat, and while Kamal shrieked and the policemen tried to drag them apart, Murad died. His knees buckled and his head flung back. He hung from his hand and his wife's hair, which had to be cut off in order to free him.

The only thing she asked for was a bath.

Chapter XXVIII

The police station had been in an uproar. Hamidah was taken roughly from her cell after having her hair hacked off to free Murad. The policeman who did the hacking, an older man named Salleh, swore he would have nightmares about it for the rest of his life and retired to a corner to drink coffee with his eyes closed. His comrades took turns sitting down next to him in silent communion.

She was placed in the interrogation room, under Rahman's watchful eye. He kept his distance lest she also come after him with a knife, but thankfully she sat quietly, calmly, softly humming under her breath. All in all, she seemed at ease, and quite pleased with her afternoon's work. She would occasionally catch Rahman's eye and give him a pleasant smile, which terrified him all the more because it seemed so natural.

Kamal remained in a state of shock, shaking and crying, unable to process what he'd seen. And who could blame him? It was an act no one should ever have to witness. The coroner who came to pronounce Murad dead – 'really dead', as he described it – gave Kamal a sedative to calm him. He looked in on Hamidah to see if she needed one, and determined she was by far the calmest person in the building. She gave him a friendly wave as he left her.

Several men, together with the cleaning staff, scrubbed the cells. There was blood everywhere – more than anyone had seen in one place outside the ritual slaughter of goats on Hari Raya Haji. And even then, it might have been a toss-up between the religious ritual and this slaughter.

* * *

Maryam was dumbstruck. She was called to the station; the officer driving the car was trembling and sweaty and refused to give any information on why she was wanted.

Upon arriving, she took in Murad's lifeless body lying on a table, covered with a sheet, awaiting transport to the hospital. She looked under the sheet: Murad was bled white, like a wax figure. She saw Salleh in the corner, and heard the sounds of mops and buckets in the cells. She peeked in the doorway and gasped at the mayhem which had left behind such blood.

Stumbling backward, she almost fell into a sobbing Kamal, but Osman grabbed her arm and led her into his office.

He spoke urgently. 'She killed him. Grabbed him through the mesh and slit his throat. *Mak Cik*, we have to question her!' And with that, he propelled her into the room where Hamidah waited.

Hamidah sat on the chair behind the table, her arm leaning against the back, her feet crossed. Her attitude was that of supreme sophistication, at odds with her newly chopped hair and filthy clothes. She smiled ruefully.

'I really should change now, shouldn't I, *Kakak*? I look a sight: a complete crazy woman. By the way, and excuse me for asking, do you have a cigarette?'

Like an automaton, Maryam offered her a pack of cigarettes, originally Mamat's, she had secreted in the folds of her sarong. She lit one for each of them. Hamidah threw her head back and blew smoke at the ceiling.

'Thank you,' she said gratefully. '*Alamak*! I can't wait to bathe. So, *Kakak*, what would you like to ask me?'

Maryam gaped at her. 'What happened to you?'

Hamidah shrugged. 'I'm out from under Murad. How many years has it been? My whole life wasted. I felt like the *pelesit* myself, kept in a bottle and fed blood. I might as well have been. And frightened? Terrified.

'It's funny now, but I can't think why. He's just a man like any other man, and now he's harmless. But for so long, I just kept my mouth shut and looked smaller and smaller so he wouldn't notice me.

'And his sister, too. What a pair. You know when I decided I had to get out?' Maryam shook her head. 'When Kamal married Hayati. If I didn't do something, he was going to become his father all over again. My sweet little boy. I couldn't let it happen.'

'But why ...?'

'Kill him?' Hamidah finished helpfully. 'It was the only way to escape. Otherwise I'd always fear he'd come after me. I was so trapped! My parents wouldn't help me, they were thrilled with the marriage. A prestigious family and lots of money. It's such a shortsighted view.

'Well, I can't blame them for thinking that at first. But they should have helped me, taken me home. They knew how evil he was, but they wanted me to stay.

'I always liked Aziz. I thought he would have been a much nicer husband ... well, anyone would. That's why I wanted Kamal to marry his daughter, the younger one. Then he'd be out of his father's influence. I thought Aziz would want to have my son in his family, you know, as a remembrance of me. So we would be joined in the end; you know, the same grandchildren.'

She sighed regretfully. 'I was wrong, it seems. He didn't want anything to do with Murad, not that I blame him, and he certainly didn't want grandchildren with Murad's blood.

'Well, before I could do anything about it, poor Kamal was married to Yati. She's just like her mother: *salin tak tumpah,* not a drop spilled, and this is not a good thing. She'll drive him crazy. I've already asked him to divorce her.'

She tapped the ashes on the floor. Maryam didn't dare interrupt: she didn't even know if she could speak at all.

'I was jealous, you know,' she added, conversationally. 'Jamillah had Aziz, her girls, her job at the market. I mean, a normal life. And I was locked up with Murad and his familiar. Can you imagine?'

She removed another cigarette from the pack. 'About six months after we got married, he started talking about this *pelesit*. It was enough to make me crazy for real. A grasshopper in a bottle. He fed it blood, and he wanted me to feed it blood, too. But do you know what I did? I always changed the grasshopper.' she finished triumphantly. 'He thought it was the same bug for years and years. No, I let it go and caught another one. That was my revenge: catching grasshoppers. It isn't a life.

'And it wasn't even a real *pelesit*! Just a grasshopper. A harmless grasshopper. And he thought he knew so much about black magic.' She laughed raucously. It was as if this was her final triumph. 'You should never confuse plain meanness with black magic. It's a good thing to remember.'

'What happened to your hair?' She couldn't believe that was her first question, but she could not drag her eyes away from hair which looked like it had been hacked off with a machete. As it turned out, it had.

'I know, it looks awful,' Hamidah said mournfully. 'You know, Murad grabbed my hair through that mesh on top of the wall and started banging my head against the bricks.' Now Maryam noticed the bruises along the side of her head, which was also swelling.

'You need some ice,' she said automatically. Osman went to the door. 'And then?'

'I must have twisted and his hand got tangled. It was all matted, you know.' She patted what was left of her locks. 'Then I stabbed him and slit his throat. And he died, of course, and his hand was still in my hair. He was hanging off it, really, and it hurt! And I couldn't move, so one of the policemen very kindly cut it off to get me free of him.'

'The knife?' Maryam gulped. She couldn't seem to put together a full sentence.

'Oh that. It was hidden, in my underwear. Because you never know.'

'Indeed not.'

She turned to Osman. 'So you see, I couldn't let anyone bathe me. They'd take away my knife, and I was saving it to kill him.'

'Of course.'

Maryam felt she would never be able to get the stunned look from her face, or keep her jaw from hanging open.

'Did you ... Jamillah?' Maryam could barely form the words.

Hamidah interpreted this correctly. 'Did I kill her? Certainly not!' Her expression implied it was Maryam who might well be the crazy one. 'Murad did,' she explained calmly.

'What?'

'Oh yes. He smothered her with a towel.'

'How do you know?'

'How would I know?' she replied tartly. 'He told me.'

Maryam turned to look at Osman in wonderment. She couldn't believe what she was hearing.

'Surely you suspected,' Hamidah continued, unperturbed. 'I know Aziz thought it was Murad who did it – to exact some kind of revenge. For what exactly, I don't think he knew. But that was Murad all over, just revenge without any reason for it.

'I think, and of course,' she said confidentially, 'it's just my opinion, that Murad wanted to get back at him for the fight over the boat. He thought everyone should happily accept whatever he gave them and be grateful. You've never seen anyone so mad as he was after that fight.'

She shook her head, remembering. 'Too bad he didn't fall and break his neck.' She shrugged, a what-can-you-do gesture.

'But how did he ...?'

'Kill her? I just told you! Everyone knew there would be a *main puteri*. He went to the *kampong* and then ...'

'Alone?'

'What?'

'Was he alone?'

Now Hamidah was not nearly as chatty. 'I don't know,' she said thoughtfully, as though trying to recall an event long ago. 'I don't know who might have been there with him.'

'Kamal?' Maryam suggested, speaking very softly.

'Kamal? No.' She clamped her mouth shut as though she might never open it again.

'But he came with you to my *kampong*?'

'I'm his mother. I needed his help!'

'To do what?'

'*Kakak* ...' She leaned on the table and snaked another cigarette out of the box. She looked up and turned again to Osman, eyes downcast and a small, polite smile on her lips. 'May I have some coffee, please?'

He got up, whispered through the door and came back with ice in a towel, which Hamidah applied to her head with murmured thanks. He settled himself in his chair, looking at the prisoner expectantly. She took a deep drag on her cigarette.

'*Kakak*,' she repeated, 'Murad didn't like you, I'm afraid.'

Maryam smothered her amusement, it simply wouldn't do for her to laugh out loud now. 'Did you think it would bother me?'

'Oh, not at all, not at all,' she waved her cigarette in the air. 'But if he didn't like you, it was a very short distance to harming you. I know it! He might think of sending his grasshopper after you,' she smirked, greatly enjoying her final joke on him. 'Or he might help the grasshopper. You annoyed him.'

'How?' Maryam asked, though she could easily guess.

'Well, let me see.' She counted on her fingers, cigarette held firmly between her lips. 'You work in the market. You talk to people, even men. You talked to him!

'And, you were helping the police, and he told me you had no right to. *Membuang garam kelaut,* he said: the police using you was like throwing salt into the ocean. You were just pretending to be important, and the police would never listen to you.'

Maryam was insulted, even given the source.

'He didn't know what he was talking about,' Osman's mild, flat-accented voice was firm. '*Mak Cik* Maryam is the police force's greatest asset!'

Maryam smiled at him, grateful that he came immediately to her defence, even if he was defending her against a lunatic.

'You've convinced me your husband didn't like me. Not a problem. But *Kakak*, it wasn't your husband climbing into my window, it was Kamal, and you were there.'

'Oh that.' She seemed supremely indifferent. 'Well, you know, Kamal is his son.'

Maryam stayed silent, her eyebrows raised, awaiting clarification.

'Well, he told him to go! Can't you see that? Kamal would never have done such a thing on his own. He's not like that.'

Maryam and Osman looked at each other. Kamal seemed very much like that indeed.

'And …?' Osman prompted.

Now Hamidah seemed exasperated. 'So Murad *told* him to go. And Kamal, he's a good boy, he told me where he was going. Murad told him to climb in and smother you, in the same way Jamillah died. Then it would look like this happened every time there was a *main puteri* in Kampong Penambang. It's clever when you think about it. I hated him, but he could be clever.'

'It wasn't that clever, since everyone was expecting it – and it didn't work,' Maryam pointed out.

'Well, as I told you, Kamal is not that kind of boy. He really didn't want to do it, so he made sure he got caught.'

'I'm not sure about that at all, *Mak Cik*,' Osman interjected. 'He seemed pretty determined.'

'I was there too,' she replied loftily. 'If Kamal really wanted it done, it would have been.'

'Don't even argue,' Maryam advised him. 'There isn't any reason.' Osman shrugged, and frowned at his notebook.

'So you see,' Hamidah continued, believing she had won that round, 'Kamal was just going through the motions so he wouldn't have disobeyed his father. Who, I can tell you now, was waiting not far away to see if everything was done correctly. But he must have heard the commotion, so he ran back to Semut Api, the coward, and left us two with the police.'

'I see.'

'I needed to dress this way,' she said earnestly, 'so you would think I was completely crazy.

'It worked,' Osman assured her.

'See? I wanted to make sure you saw that my son didn't mean it, that he was innocent.'

'I'm not sure I'm following you,' Osman said politely. She ignored him.

'You must let Kamal go,' she instructed him. 'Because he didn't do anything, and Murad killed Jamillah and now he's dead too, so you see, it all works out.' She smiled broadly at them both. 'I've solved it for you.' And she looked around, awaiting the grateful thanks she reckoned she deserved.

Chapter XXIX

Maryam insisted on leaving the station and walking over to the market, where they could sit at Rubiah's counter and consider what they'd just heard. 'I couldn't stay there a moment longer,' she told Rubiah when they had settled. 'It looks like ... well, I don't even know what it looks like. It's covered in blood. I don't think Murad had any left in him.'

Rubiah gasped. 'How did it ...? Why?'

Maryam shrugged and looked over at Osman to give the details, such as they were. Rubiah turned pale as she heard the details, then sat down heavily on her stool. '*Astigfirullah*!' she breathed.

'But I think she's lying.' Maryam told them. 'It's so convenient to blame Murad for it now that he's dead. And she hates him anyway, so she's not looking to honour his memory. I think both these families think their children did it, and they're trying to shield them.

'Kamal?'

'Of course. He came in my window, why not Jamillah's? That poor kid has the wrong parents.'

'Well, I certainly like that better than Zaiton.'

Maryam nodded, her thoughts far away. 'Not that it matters who you want it to be. If that's the basis, then we have the murderer and he's already dead. Very convenient.'

'Yes, it's too bad,' Rubiah said. 'But,' she brightened, 'just because she's crazy, doesn't mean she isn't telling the truth. Maybe it was Murad,' she ended hopefully.

'More likely Kamal,' Maryam told her.

Rubiah made a disappointed moue and went back to stacking coffee cups. 'What now?'

'Kamal, I guess.

* * *

Before Maryam could actually leave her own yard to head off to the police station, Zaiton and her father accosted her. Zaiton had clearly been weeping: her face was damp, red, puffy, her eyes nearly closed and her nose stuffed. 'What's the matter?' Maryam asked, concerned. Had she lost the baby?

'Zaiton and I, we ...' Aziz didn't seem able to quite get it out. 'That is, we came to speak to you.' He looked tired, now that she looked more closely; in fact, he looked completely wrung out.

'Come up, please. And you look like you could use some coffee and something to eat.'

As they entered the living room, Zaiton sniffling loudly, Maryam asked Aliza to serve. Her hair was now in a bob, sleek and thick, and if still somewhat shorter than she would have chosen, it was nothing to stare at with pity.

Zaiton looked at Aliza and began wailing. She was saying something, Maryam was sure of it, but couldn't understand a word. She waved Aliza into the kitchen with a look telling her food was a top priority. Aliza quickly scampered down the stairs, relieved not to be listening to Zaiton, whatever her problems were.

'Now, you just calm down now and tell me what's the matter.'

Maryam reminded herself that this girl no longer had a mother, and she fought down her impatience to be done with this. The right thing, the neighbourly thing to do would be to provide the maternal advice she clearly needed so sorely. She patted Zaiton on the back and encouraged her to speak.

'I did it.'

'You did what?'

Zaiton choked, and Maryam handed her some tissues.

'Tell me, Zaiton. I can't help you if you won't.'

She looked inquiringly at Aziz, who was examining his hands. Aliza and Yi came in with steaming hot sweet tea, chocolates, and a heaping plate of cookies. They both stood there, watching Zaiton quizzically; Aliza shrugged minimally and started pouring.

'Drink this,' Maryam ordered her when the choking sobs subsided. 'And have a cookie.' She heard herself with amusement, she sounded just like Rubiah.

Zaiton held the cup in two hands and looked up at Maryam. 'I killed my mother.'

'What?'

'She did,' Aziz said tiredly. He looked like a man who was

finished with living. 'That's why we came. To tell you.'

'I … What?'

Zaiton nodded. 'I didn't mean to. But I did.'

'What happened?'

'Oh, *Mak Cik*, just take me and put me in jail. I can't even live with myself.'

'Tell me what you did.'

She sniffed and wiped her eyes. 'When she went to sleep and I wanted to talk to her, I … I pushed her.'

'Off the bed?'

'No, on the bed, but she rolled over on her stomach. And I think that's when she suffocated.'

'Why didn't you roll her back?'

'I was mad because she didn't talk to me. So I just left her there and went out.' She put her head in her hands.

'Was she not able to move?'

'She was sleeping.'

'She'd just fallen asleep?'

Zaiton nodded.

'Do you think she would have been able to move while she was sleeping?'

'Not if she was suffocating.'

'You know,' Maryam said gently, 'you really have to hold something over their face to suffocate anyone. Not just have them roll over.'

Aziz cut in. 'Thank you, *Kakak*. You're trying to see the best of it, and I appreciate what you're doing. But we, our family, can't live with this anymore, hiding the truth like that. It was an accident, and I don't think Zaiton meant to do it.'

He put both hands over his face for a moment before continuing. 'I will stand by my daughter,' his voice was thick with tears. 'We'll get a good lawyer. She didn't mean it, but she did what she did.'

'But we don't know ...'

'We're going to the police station to turn ourselves in. I hope they'll let her come home, being in her condition, you know. But I don't know ...' His attention wandered, and he seemed unable to focus.

'I'll come with you – to help,' Maryam reassured him. 'We'll see what can be done.'

Maryam managed to get Osman alone before Aziz and Zaiton could confess.

'I don't know if she did it,' she told him urgently. 'I mean, I just don't know. She feels so guilty for having left her sleeping on her stomach – what she's going to do when the baby comes I can't imagine. But even if that's what killed her, it wasn't intentional.'

She shook her head sadly. 'This poor family is just beside itself. Do you think you could let her go home instead of staying in that jail with Hamidah?' She shuddered. 'She's having a baby after all, and Hamidah is ... let's say, unusual right now.'

Osman nodded. He looked exhausted himself. 'Let me talk to them. She can't stay here now. Nobody should have to stay here after what's happened. Even I don't like it.' He gave her a wan smile and left to meet the two standing at the desk.

Maryam watched from his office as he took them into his

room. The last two days had been like a preview of hell.

* * *

In ways no one could adequately elucidate, the news of Zaiton's confession spread through Kampong Penambang immediately, and when Maryam returned from the police station, surely no more than an hour after she'd left, everyone already knew.

Her neighbours were gathered outside in small knots of people, shaking their heads with the inexplicable evil of it all. Mothers wondered at the unnatural order of things, and people who would never have mentioned the timing of Zaiton's baby now murmured about it as an illustration of just how far off the rails the girl had gone. Pregnant before marriage, killing her own mother; it was as though she were possessed by the devil himself.

Rahim had gone back to his family in Semut Api, escaping the scrutiny the family could expect to come under. He pleaded with his parents to allow Zaiton to come and stay with them when she came back from the station, or got out of jail, whichever came first. But they counselled him instead to divorce her that very evening, and when the baby arrived, to take it from her immediately and raise it with the help of his parents. Or better yet, a new wife.

His mother pointed out ominously that a girl who would kill her mother might easily kill her child; obviously, she had crossed all boundaries of acceptable human behaviour and was now operating in the shady area peopled by *jinn* and evil spirits.

And what of this child, she mused. Would it be a normal human child, or a supernatural one with a taste for blood and matricide? Perhaps, his father suggested, Zaiton was a *jinn* herself, which would explain a great deal, and Rahim had barely escaped with his own life before she turned on him. None of this described the wife Rahim knew, and it all frightened him. He refused to divorce her and went to sleep rather than speak to anyone further.

* * *

In the market the next morning, Maryam found a tearful and frightened Zainab at her stall, pale and tired. She tried to comfort her, assuring her it would be alright.

'And anyway, I'm not convinced it was Zaiton at all,' Maryam stated with more confidence than she actually felt. After all, her reason for doubting it was only that it was unthinkable to believe it true, and she knew this was inadequate at best, and dangerous for everyone at worst. Still, it was not a time to air her doubts to this distraught sister.

Zainab folded her arms on the counter of Maryam's stall and buried her head in them. 'He's divorcing me,' she said, her voice strangled and muffled by her arms.

'What? Zainab, I can't hear you at all.'

She raised her tear-stained face and blew her nose on an offered tissue. 'He's divorcing me,' she sobbed. 'Because my sister's an evil murderer, and we might all be ... polluted.' She commenced wailing again. Rashidah came to investigate from the stall next door.

'What happened?' Rashidah's brows were drawn up, and she patted Zainab firmly on the back, as you would a baby you wanted to burp.

'My husband's divorcing me because my sister killed our mother,' she choked. 'He doesn't want anything to do with our family anymore!' And once again, she dissolved.

'*Alamak*! She killed her own mother?'

Maryam shrugged, then nodded slightly. 'She's confessed to it. But I don't know, maybe she didn't really … It's hard to know the truth,' she admitted. 'But divorcing poor Zainab! That's just not fair.'

'Look what's she's done!' Zainab drew breath and steeled herself for another speech. 'Running away to get married, and I had to go all the way to Patani to get her! And then I had to make sure our father was alright, and have the *kenduri*, and now this. She's possessed!' she told Rashidah. 'She's ruining my life!'

'I know it seems like that now …' Rashidah struggled to seem optimistic.

'It doesn't seem like it,' Zainab corrected her. 'It is it. Look what's happened to us – to me, my kids. Oh *Mak Cik*,' she implored, 'Can't you help me?' And a bout of fresh tears quickly commenced.

'I'll do my best,' Maryam declared stoutly. 'And *Mak Cik* Rubiah will help also …' As though summoned, she straight away appeared at Maryam's elbow.

'*Mak Cik* Rubiah will help what?'

'Poor Zainab,' Rashidah explained. 'Her husband wants to divorce her because of Zaiton killing their mother …'

'Allegedly,' Maryam reminded her.

Rashidah rolled her eyes at Rubiah.

'I heard about it. She confessed?'

Maryam nodded, unwilling to raise her voice over Zainab's cries.

Rubiah shook her head slowly. 'I don't even know what to say.'

'She thinks she pushed her over on her stomach and she suffocated.'

Rubiah raised her eyebrows. 'Are you sure that's all she did?'

'I'm not sure about anything anymore. I'm just hoping it isn't true; any of it.'

'My poor mother,' Zainab gasped. She would make herself sick with all this crying, Maryam thought. This kind of raw emotion, call it hysteria, opened the sufferer to all kinds of spirit invasion. It was dangerous on many levels. Maintaining a calm equilibrium was most conducive to health, both physical and mental.

Though Zainab certainly had reason for tears, in the end it would harm her, and possibly the rest of them. And Zainab was a mother, whose children might be facing a most difficult time. She owed it to them to keep her wits about her. Maryman told her so.

Zainab nodded, so swollen from tears, it was difficult for her to breathe. 'Your right, of course, *Mak Cik*. I'll try to control myself ...'

'Where is your father?'

'At home, I think.'

'Rahim?'

'Gone back to Semut Api.'

'Has he ...?'

‘No, I don’t think so. He loves Zaiton. But,’ she reflected, ‘I’m sure his parents will advise him to get a divorce. They’ll be afraid of Zaiton and what she’ll do to them. Who wants a girl who’s killed her mother?’

Who indeed?

Chapter XXX

Marriage negotiations were notoriously delicate discussions, offence could be easily given or taken. Maryam had put them off until she felt herself strong again and up to the challenge of oblique and metaphorical speech which, while indirect, would still be understood by all who heard it.

And she was up to it now; the family delegation was leaving for Kedai Buluh, to at last speak to Rosnah's parents about marriage. Maryam and Mamat, Ashikin and Daud, Rubiah and Dollah were ready to meet Malek and Zahara and converge upon Rosnah's family. Maryam worried there were too many of them.

'Do you think they'll be overwhelmed when we come in? We're such a big group.'

'They'll have all their relatives there too,' Mamat assured her, fussing with his *songkok*, a black velvet brimless hat worn with traditional Malay clothing, pushing it forward and backward on his head, testing it for best effect. 'Their house will be packed.'

Maryam decided on the extra bangle. She'd been debating it, wanting to look prosperous, but not so prosperous that the family would demand an exorbitant bride price or too lavish an array of gifts. Maryam and Mamat had discussed it, and they wanted to provide clothes and jewellery which were as generous as they could afford to be, keeping in mind they'd be doing it again in a few years with Yi.

However nervous she was, Maryam was also confident that Rosnah's family were in circumstances much like their own, and inclined to be reasonable. Malek had smoothed the way for negotiations, having had a quiet word with Rosnah's father, a distant relative of Zahara's. All was now in place.

Ashikin and Daud arrived first, as friends of the prospective bride, and the two girls withdrew to a bedroom to discuss the negotiations. Traditionally, Rosnah would have peeped at the conclave from behind a door, or maybe entered to serve refreshments. She would be serving today, allowing the in-laws to get a good look at her, so they would not *membeli kerbau ditengah padang:* buy a buffalo in the middle of a field. The traditional rules would be observed, though nowadays, with girls going to school and knowing each other's friends, it was hardly the mystery it had been in times gone by.

The full complement of Azmi's family arrived, as did the home team, and Mamat's forecast was correct: the house was crammed with people, all wearing their best with their most refined manners on show. Rosnah served the refreshments, and all Maryam's kinfolk smiled beneficently upon her and thanked her profusely. When she and Ashikin had retired to the kitchen, Mamat cleared his throat and began his prepared remarks.

The whole business was approached indirectly, so as to avoid embarrassment to either side should the negotiations ultimately be unsuccessful. It provided plausible deniability to the participants, who could claim to be discussing some other, wholly innocuous matter, and not marriage.

In this vein, various remarks were exchanged: first, fathers and uncles, then mothers and aunts, taking turns, adding their own literary flourishes. Behind the game, however, serious business was being conducted, and, finally all were satisfied that the deal was, in principle, agreed. The details on money and gifts would be discussed at another time by a representative from each side.

After oceans of coffee and mountains of rice cakes, Maryam and the full entourage left, thrilled at their skill and luck in carrying off such a delicate matter, more convinced than ever that Rosnah was the perfect wife for Azmi and his sister marvellously clever to have thought of it and bringthe union to fruition.

Ashikin called Azmi later to give him the results, and to remind him again that it had been her idea. It would improve his character to realize how much she'd done for him.

The *enam sembilan* mark, a distinctive braided robe indentation on Maryam's forehead, was fading, but she believed she would forever see it there. She examined herself in the mirror when she took off her headscarf, and so far had not dared to leave the house without that scarf. Mamat swore it now looked like a faint red mark, completely unnoticeable, and she was ready to go out as she had before. But the image of how it looked at the beginning swam before her eyes, and she thought everyone else's eyes were immediately drawn to it, so she kept herself swathed.

Aziz's clear belief in Zaiton's guilt led Maryam to confront him, now buoyed by the success of marriage negotiations. He was sitting on the porch of his house, looking woebegone, and she greeted him, trying to be cheerful and optimistic about Zaiton's possible innocence.

He shook his head. 'Thank you, *Kakak*, I know what you're trying to do. But it doesn't matter anymore. We're finished here.'

'Is Zainab ...?'

'No, not yet. But the longer this goes on, the more likely it is. Rahim's parents want him to divorce Zaiton. I don't think he wants to, but I also think he will ... after a while. And why not?' he asked hopelessly.

'Do you think she did it, *Abang*?'

He nodded quietly. 'I don't think she meant to, but it happened.'

'But what if *Kakak* Jamillah just went to sleep and someone slipped in afterward and killed her? And Zaiton is completely innocent?'

'I can't make myself believe it.'

Maryam watched as he seemed to crumble in front of her. The whole family was now in ruins. She could hardly bear thinking about it.

'*Abang*,' she asked suddenly, 'Have you suspected it might have been Zaiton for a while?'

'Why?'

'Did you?'

'What are you really asking me?'

She wasn't quite sure how to say it. 'I wondered whether ... you know, when you thought she might have been guilty, to protect her, did you ...?'

'Hit you over the head?'

She blushed. How crude of her, how wrong to ask a man in his situation.

'Yes,' he said tiredly. 'I did it, *Kakak*. I wanted you to stop looking into this, so I could keep my daughter and grandchild.

'It was wrong,' he continued, 'and it was wrong to ignore Jamillah that way, but I ... maybe I wasn't thinking. In fact, I'm sure of it. I'm sorry.' He hung his head.

'Oh.' She wondered what the appropriate comment for her would be. *Never mind? I forgive you? How could you?* All would do, and yet none struck her as really fitting. He might have killed her; he certainly wounded her and made her sick for what seemed like the longest time.

She touched her headscarf briefly, when would she be able to stop wearing it? She hated being bound up in it, but feared people seeing the mark and laughing at her. 'But you really hurt me,' she blurted out, 'I still have the mark ...'

'I know.' He didn't pick up his head.

'And with an *enam sembilan*,' she continued, picking up steam, 'which leaves such a bruise. Why would you do that? You've known me for how long? And you still didn't mind nearly killing me?' Her anger was rising now.

'You're right,' he agreed.

'You're not even listening to me now,' she accused him. 'You're just waiting for me to finish.'

'What can I say? I said I was sorry, and I am. I can't do anything else.'

She could feel her breath shortening and her face getting redder. 'This whole thing, this whole case, is about people acting without thinking. Mostly your family.' She put her hand up to her mouth, that was wrong of her to say. Rude and unnecessary. She apologized. 'I shouldn't have said that. Please forgive me.'

He shrugged. 'You're right, though. But we're being punished for it.' He paused. 'Will I go to jail now?'

'I don't know.' There was no point discussing this any further. It was time for her to go.

* * *

Both families were now destroyed. Jamillah and Murad were dead (one mourned, the other not – except for the latter's sister, who was inconsolable); Hamidah, Kamal and Zaiton were in jail and Aziz probably on his way; Zainab probably divorced, Rahim fled to Semut Api. Maryam tried to fathom how so many people could doso much wrong, or were that thoughtless.

Osman came over with Azrina, to sit on the porch and congratulate Maryam on bringing all these miscreants to justice. Azrina brought a large ripe durian, which Mamat and Yi were currently carving up in the kitchen, and Aliza served coffee.

'I love your hair,' Azrina told her. 'It looks so up-to-date!'

Aliza flashed her a brilliant smile; Azrina was right, the new style suited her and made her look more sophisticated. Aliza unobtrusively sat down just inside the doorjamb, and slowly and silently moved forward to join the group. It was a masterpiece of manoeuvring on Aliza's part. 'I don't know how we could have solved it without you, *Mak Cik*. You were the one ...'

'I don't know that we've solved it at all – yet,' Maryam admonished him. 'I'm not sure Zaiton killed her mother – it's hard to kill someone by turning them over in the bed. It takes determination, and Zaiton didn't have that.'

'Do you believe Hamidah?'

'No, but I wish I did,' Maryam said regretfully. Mamat arrived carrying a large platter of durian, which was greeted with cries of admiration. Only when the fruit had been eaten, hands washed, and cigarettes lit did the conversation return to the topic of crime.

'It's too convenient,' she told Osman. 'The murderer is dead, and Hamidah hated him. She's delighted to blacken his name now – if she knew of any other murders available, she'd accuse him of those, too.'

'Then it must be Hamidah and her son together,' Azrina said excitedly. 'Just like they were trying to get into your bedroom, *Mak Cik*, they climbed into *Mak Cik*Jamillah's before that. She can't say she never thought of it! And,' she added practically, 'she's crazy enough to do it.'

'No doubt about that,' Maryam agreed. 'You've been giving this a lot of thought.'

Azrina blushed and ducked her head. 'A little,' she admitted. 'You know, after I met Hamidah and tried to give her a bath ...' she made a face, 'I began fitting things together.' She gave Osman a guilty look. 'It's just that ... I'm interested in this kind of thing; you know, crime.'

Osman looked surprised.

'Well, I read mysteries,' she said, a touch defensively.

'Nothing wrong with that,' Maryam opined.

'And so when I knew you had this case, I just ... thought about it.'

'Well then,' Maryam said heartily, 'tell us what you've been thinking about.'

She smoothed her hair back, and tucked a stray lock behind her ear. With a careful glance at Osman, she began.

'Well, I don't know everything about it, like you do, but ...'

'The *but*. I've gotten used to it,' Osman grumbled. Maryam silenced him with a slap on the knee.

'You see, Hamidah said she was jealous of Jamillah.'

'How do you know that?'

'Didn't she say so?' she asked innocently.

'And you overheard it.'

Azrina became impatient with his questions. 'I live there!' she declared. 'I hear things when you talk about them.

'So,' she continued, 'if she felt jealous, perhaps she wanted to get rid of Jamillah and take over her life. You know: the husband, the job, the friends. All the things she felt she didn't have. And so she waited until Jamillah's house and neighborhood would be crowded with people and no one would notice one more, and then she had Kamal go to the window and smother her.'

'Why didn't anyone hear him? There were so many people sleeping in the house!'

'Because,' she said triumphantly, 'he never went in. He hung at the window, over the sill, but never went into the house. He didn't step over anyone, or walk around the house. I think he was half in the window and his mother held his feet so he wouldn't slip over. And he smothered her with a cloth, but she didn't wake because she was so tired and asleep. Maybe he even did it before *Pak Cik* Aziz went to sleep, so no one else was in the room.

'It took a lot of nerve,' she acknowledged. 'But she had more nerve than most people who aren't crazy. And maybe Kamal doesn't do a lot of thinking for himself, but just listens to what his parents tell him to do.'

'And now his wife,' Maryam added.

Azrina shrugged. 'And his wife.'

Maryam nodded. 'It all makes sense,' she said approvingly. 'The only thing to do now is talk to Kamal.

'Are you going to want to come to that too?' Osman asked her.

'No, it wouldn't be right,' she told him primly. 'I shouldn't be there. You do it.'

'Well, it's nice of you to leave it to me.'

'Don't do that,' Maryam admonished him. 'It makes you look mean.'

Chapter XXXI

While Azrina was basking in the reflected glory of her first foray into crime solving, Hamidah had been moved to the Kota Bharu jail – an insalubrious place, dark, damp and hot. It was on the outskirts of town, in the middle of empty fields. There was little thought of rehabilitation here, it was a place of punishment for wrongdoing, pure and simple.

Yet Hamidah seemed perfectly content, even given the quality of her surroundings. She sat in her cell, newly bathed, her hair still hacked and uneven. She wore a standard-issue prison sarong and a clean T-shirt, and sat happily on the bed in her cell, humming Hindi movie themes to herself and smiling at no one in particular.

Kamal was far more unhappy. The holding cells now reeked of bleach overlaying the coppery smell of blood. The walls had been scrubbed so hard the paint had dissolved, turning what had once been a bilious green into its present tone: a vile gray dripped over dirty white. His eyes stung, his throat hurt, and his mind could not take in what had happened right in front of him.

When he lay down, he saw his father hanging there, his hand

tangled in his mother's matted hair, her screaming. If it had been a horror movie, he would have said it had gone too far.

He was stretched out on the narrow cot when Osman came in to get him, lying on his stomach with his head buried in the thin, flat pillow. Even though the door slammed with a loud clang, Kamal didn't move.

'Your mother-in-law was here to see you a little while ago,' Osman told him. Kamal made a sound which could have meant 'yes', or 'no', or just a groan of anguish. 'I won't let her in to see you.'

For a minute there was no response. Then he lifted his head and said clearly, 'Thank you.'

Osman sat on the side of the cot, though there was hardly any room, and lit cigarettes for the both of them. Kamal rolled onto his side facing the wall and smoked in silence.

'Is there anything you'd like to talk to me about?'

Kamal looked at him, his face blank. 'Like what?'

'Like what happened.'

He sighed; a long, deep sigh for such a young man. 'What good would it do?'

'I'm interested.'

Osman pushed Kamal's legs out of the way so he could lean his back against the wall; it forced Kamal to sit up and do the same. He might not talk, Osman knew, but at least he couldn't bury his head. The silence dragged on for the length of one cigarette, after which Osman took out two more. He was in no rush.

'Are you just going to sit here until I say something?'

Osman nodded. '*Mak Cik* Maryam will be here soon.'

Kamal grunted 'It's terrible in here. All that bleach hurts my eyes.'

'We had to get it clean.'

'I know. But it hurts.' It was Osman's turn to grunt.

'What do you want to know?'

'Who killed *Mak Cik* Jamillah.'

'How would I know?'

'Please. Haven't we all been through enough? I can't keep up the pretence that you know nothing.' Osman was prepared to lecture him, but then thought better of it. Perhaps silence would work more effectively than a barrage of words.

Kamal appeared to fall asleep for a few minutes, while Osman contemplated which killer he preferred. Each one had something incriminating speaking against him or her, including Zaiton. But since she was pregnant, he put her last. He was staring dreamily at the wall when Maryam entered, wrinkling her nose at the ammonia which permeated the room.

'Can't we talk elsewhere?' she asked, jerking Osman out of his meditative state, and waking Kamal. They looked at her with the mild surprise of the recently woken. 'You're pretty relaxed in here, aren't you?' she asked. Kamal rubbed his eyes and ran his hand through his hair, as she ushered them out into the interrogation room. 'I can't take the fumes,' she explained.

'Neither can I,' Kamal admitted. 'It feels so good to get out of there.'

Maryam arranged her cigarettes and coffee in front of her and looked up at Kamal, who sat in his chair, half stupefied, his eyes heavy, his hair dishevelled.

'Tell me, Kamal,' she began matter-of-factly, 'was that the first time you climbed through a bedroom window?'

'What?' He looked mystified.

'When my husband caught you coming into our window – was it the first time you'd ever done it?'

'I'd never been to your house before!' he protested.

'That's not what I'm asking you. Had you ever done something similar? Climbed in through *other* windows, perhaps.'

He shook his head like a dog coming out of water. 'No, why?'

'Was that the first time you went on an expedition like that with your mother?'

He nodded, but seemed unsure of the answer.

'Alright.' Maryam had four children, and was well-versed in the need to ask a particular question in just the right way so as to get to the heart of the matter. She honed in on specifics, in a way that any of the four children would immediately recognize as trouble.

'With either of your parents, your mother or your father?'

He looked at Osman for assistance. Osman kept his eyes trained on Maryam.

'Well, of course, I'd been in Kampong Penambang ...'

'Kamal!' He jumped. 'You know what I'm asking you, so stop pretending you don't. Did you go with your father to *Mak Cik* Jamillah's house after the *main puteri*?'

'No.'

'No?'

'No,' he said firmly, now sure of his answer. 'I didn't.'

She backed up, sensing an opening. 'Did you go to her house

at the time?'

He was silent.

'You did go, but not with your father,' she surmised. 'You went with your mother. Your father never had anything to do with this. He didn't even know about it. I'm right, aren't I?'

His eyes cast anxiously between Osman and Maryam, as though trying to decide which was safer. He seemed to realize neither was safe, and he began squirming in his seat.

'Your mother said your father killed *Mak Cik* Jamillah, but now I'm going to guess your *mother* went to her house that night. And you went with her, because she asked for your help.'

He looked terrified. 'I didn't …'

'Did your mother?'

'Did she … what?'

Maryam let out a sigh of exasperation. 'I don't mind telling you I'm getting tired of this,' she informed him. 'You and your mother are driving me mad. Now answer me, or you can stay in that cell until you're an old man. It won't bother me.'

She gave him a minute to digest this threat. 'Did your mother go to *Mak Cik* Jamillah's house after the *main puteri*? Yes or no?' They all waited.

'She may have,' he admitted. No one moved or spoke.

He then amended that testimony: 'I think so.' The silence not only continued, it grew more ominous.

'You know, she got ideas into her head, and you couldn't talk her out of them. I had to go to see what she was doing, to protect her from herself, you might say.' He now examined the plaid on his sarong. 'I just followed her to make sure she didn't get into trouble.'

Maryam's expression plainly read 'really?' Kamal gulped and continued.

'I was behind her. There were so many people, I kind of lost her in the crowd. I walked around the house to see if she was there, and I saw her, she was walking away, on her way home already. So I jumped up onto the sill, just to look in.'

'And?' Osman prompted?

'And *Mak Cik* Jamillah was lying there facing the wall, and she was already dead. I touched her! That's how I knew she wasn't asleep.'

'So it was your mother who killed her, then?' Osman asked, relieved at last to have come to the conclusion.

He shook his head. 'She was already cold.'

Maryam and Osman exchanged dumbfounded looks. 'How long had you been in the *kampong* by then?'

He shrugged. 'Maybe fifteen minutes or so.'

'And your mother?'

'Maybe five minutes more.'

'Now, were you at home when she left so you could follow her?'

'I was in Kampong Tikat, at my house.' He then adjusted this statement. No, at *Mak Su* Noriah's house.'

'And your mother stopped by?'

He shook his head. 'She didn't like *Mak Su* Noriah.' This was one of the first truly sane things Maryam had heard about Hamidah.

'So how did you know she was going?'

'She'd talked about it before. About watching the *main puteri*. She didn't think *Mak Cik* Jamillah had anything to be sick about. She was kind of angry about it.'

'Angry?'

'She thought *Mak Cik* Jamillah had a pretty good life, much happier than her own. So she envied her, you see, and didn't, or couldn't, understand why she wasn't happy. I knew that; she'd talked about it before.'

'For a long time?'

He shook his head. 'Well, a lot more in the last couple of years, I guess. Before I got married and moved away.'

'And that was the reason you went to Kampong Penambang? Because you thought you might find your mother there? So really, you didn't follow her so much as went to find her there.'

He shrugged. 'I followed her there. I got there when the *main puteri* had just ended.'

'How do you know?'

'The musicians were still putting their things away. So it couldn't have been too long, right?'

Now it was Maryam's turn to shrug.

Perhaps she shouldn't have spoken with *Pak* Nik Lah about the case, he was a civilian (though to be fair, so was she) and not privy to the details of crime in Kelantan. But she was impressed with his knowledge of people, and his shrewd assessment of them, and decided that his role as a *bomoh* offered some privilege of confidentiality.

She watched him on the porch with Mamat and Aliza from

inside the house, how his mere presence seemed to put everyone at ease. More than anyone else, he might have the insight to cut through this knot of lies, half-lies and delusions.

'I've just come to check on my patients,' he told her with a grin when he arrived. 'But I see they're hardly patients any more. Aliza! Look at you!'

Aliza smiled shyly, but with her old spark, and Mamat felt his eyes tear when he thought how close he had come to losing her.

By this point, Maryam had stepped out on the porch to join them.

'*Kakak*,' *Pak* Nik Lah continued, 'why are you still wearing that scarf? Is the mark really still there?'

Maryam mumbled something unintelligible even to herself, then backed into the house for the obligatory coffee. She still hated to be reminded of the scar, and refused to let anyone look at her forehead. But when she returned, *Pak* Nik Lah reached over, after apologizing, and lifted the scarf as Maryam froze. 'There's nothing here,' he told her gently. 'It's all gone.' He smiled. 'You can take it off now.'

She thought to argue, or make excuses to leave it where it was, but then took heart and untied it. Mamat brightened up and laughed with pleasure seeing her without it, and Aliza assured her there was nothing to see.

'You look so much better this way,' Yi concurred. 'You look like yourself again.' She smiled modestly, and reflexively put her hand to her head.

'Don't do that, *Mak*,' Aliza chided her. 'There isn't anything there.'

She asked *Pak* Nik Lah if she could discuss the case with him, since he had cured Jamillah as well as herself, and would naturally have an interest.

The three adults drew closer, and Maryam explained about their flock of confessed felons.

The *bomoh* was startled, having understood the problem was more commonly the opposite – much suspicion and no one coming forward, rather than many coming forward but none, somehow, looking guilty enough. Yet he thought he understood the motivations of each one.

Zaiton could not forgive herself for her pregnancy, and believed it worsened her mother's condition. Fighting with her mother made it so much the worse.

Hamidah, well, she wanted only to kill Murad, and once he was dead, why not blame him for any other convenient crime? All of these made sense, he announced.

As for Aziz attacking her, it was shameful, but as he had said many times, Aziz was a troubled man. However – and he would not want this misconstrued – Aziz may improve now, with Murad gone. Perhaps he would make peace with his losses, and stop brooding.

Pak Nik Lah's opinion was that his brooding was detrimental to his health overall; weren't they all familiar with *amok?* It began with brooding, deep and incessant, and then developed into indiscriminate killing.

They all nodded sagely. Of course, they knew about that phenonenon, but hadn't thought about Aziz as being on the cusp of any such outburst.

That was the horror of *amok*, *Pak* Nik Lah explained, no one knew it was coming until havoc had already been wreaked. Aziz's foray into wielding the *enam sembilan* was, in his professional opinion, a minor eruption of the state, one in which the sufferer lost control over his impulses and became murderous.

Maryam and Mamat were sobered by this diagnosis, wondering if Aziz might have had the same problem with Jamillah. As though he read their minds, *Pak* Nik Lah advised that he thought not. The hallmark of amok was uncontrolled violence; whoever killed Jamillah was controlled, careful and cautious. It had been planned, with a great deal of nerve, he thought, not blundered into in a rage. Therefore, he added, it was far more frightening.

Maryam considered the description just given – it sounded like Hamidah. She ticked off the attributes *Pak* Nik Lah had listed: nerve? Absolutely. Hamidah was fearless when she was on a mission.

Cautious? Life with Murad had made her cautious and cunning, planning for the long term without giving away any clues. *Cencaru makan petang:* the horse mackerel feeds late in the day, but it eats well in the end. Of course, that could also describe Murad, another impassive face on a simmering temper.

But as Maryam believed, Murad channelled his venom through his familiar, to keep his own hands clean. Hamidah wouldn't mind getting her hands dirty. *Pak* Nik Lah nodded, and concurred. It made sense.

'Then do you think Hamidah killed her?'

'She's certainly capable of it.'

'Would she have put the plan together and had Kamal actually carry it out.'

Pak Nik Lah sighed, and leaned back against the porch railing. 'She might. But she'd never admit it.'

'Kamal might, if he was involved.'

'Would it be so terrible,' Mamat asked diffidently, 'if Hamidah was guilty? Whether she did it herself or asked someone else to actually do it for her, she was the planner behind it. She admits it. Why not just leave it at that?'

Maryam looked at him sadly. 'It would be nice if we could just decide who would be the least ... destructive. But I can't.'

'Kamal makes the most sense,' *Pak* Nik Lah suggested gently. 'He'd do what his mother told him, no matter how odd it might seem. I don't know how he is now with his wife, but at heart, he's easily led.'

'You've met his wife,' Maryam said when she could trust herself not to giggle. 'I think it's safe to say he's easily led there too. I hope his wife isn't advising him to kill anyone.'

* * *

Maryam and Rubiah were escorted into the Kota Bharu prison by Osman and Rahman. And a good thing, too, since it allowed them to avoid the visitors' line. The women waiting to visit were much poorer, more ragged than Maryam and Rubiah. Most were painfully thin, wrapped in torn and faded sarongs, with T-shirts rather than *baju kurung*. They stood with their arms folded, their feet placed far apart in worn plastic flip-flops. Many chewed betel quids, with teeth black and lips stained bright red, leaning over every so often to spit. Indeed, the ground beside the wall where they stood was mottled with old betel stains. A few smoked home-rolled cigarettes. All looked resigned, even hopeless, and shuffled slowly forward as the line moved in infinitesimal increments.

A cottage industry selling snack and drinks to the lines of visitors waiting there had grown up, mostly on the back of three-wheeled bicycles, whose riders plied their trade up and down the line. The two *mak cik* drew stares from the rest of the women, but none commented or spoke to them; they remained silent, save for the occasional sound of spit and the shuffling of feet.

The room they were placed in was as horrible as the rest of the prison, and exuded despair and defeat. It was dark, and dreadfully hot, with a thick layer of grime over the stained grey walls and floors. Yet when she was brought in, Hamidah fairly glowed with contentment and smiled as graciously as if she were overseeing a party in her own home.

'How nice to see you!' She beamed around the room and patted Maryam's arm. 'So thoughtful of you to come to visit. And in this heat!'

Maryam forced a smile. 'How are you feeling?'

'Oh fine. Not as nice as being home, of course, but I'm happy enough.' She certainly looked serene. She lowered her voice. 'Do you have a cigarette? There are so few little luxuries here! Not that I'm complaining.'

Maryam slid her home-rolled cigarettes across the table, and Hamidah gratefully took one before speaking again. 'How can I help you? You look like you came here for a reason.'

She may have been crazy, but she wasn't simple; she could be a formidable opponent, as her husband discovered too late. Maryam tried to tread carefully, and not give too much away. 'Just seeing how you are,' she replied. She looked benign, but Hamidah was not fooled.

She smiled at her cigarette, not looking up. 'Ah, still looking for someone to blame for Jamillah's death, are you? You don't like Murad as the murderer? Why not?'

Maryam was flustered to be called out so bluntly. Rubiah answered for her. '*Kakak*, like it or not, I just wonder whether Murad actually was involved in that crime. Not that I'm disagreeing ...'

'But you are,' she answered sweetly. 'And he did do it, you know, so I'm wondering why.'

'No one actually saw him in our *kampong* when Jamillah died.'

'It must have been such a crowd! And as I told you before, he was clever. Mean, though.' She looked thoughtful and leaned back in her chair, enjoying her cigarette.

'Someone saw you, though.'

'Me?' She laughed. 'I wasn't there.'

'I understand you were.'

'*Kakak*, how can it be?'

'Kamal says you were. He said he followed you.' Hamidah fell silent, considering how to respond.

'*Kakak*?' Maryam asked, prodding her for an answer.

She lifted up her head. 'Kamal is mistaken.'

Rubiah shook her head. 'I don't think so.'

'Kamal is confused.'

'No.'

'I know my own boy. He's confused.'

'I don't want to keep arguing this all day. He says you were there, and he followed you there, and he saw you come down from the sill.'

'*Me*?' She laughed again, a little more forced this time. 'An old woman like me climbing into windows? It doesn't seem very likely, does it?'

'However unlikely, that's what he says.'

'Poor boy,' Hamidah crooned. 'You must have done some terrible things to him to make him say that.'

'I did not!' Maryam was offended.

'Maybe not you, *Kakak*,' she replied, unimpressed by Maryam's high dudgeon, 'but someone did.' She skewed her eyes towards Osman, startled to suddenly find himself in the role of Grand Inquisitor.

'He didn't either,' Maryam retorted. '*Kakak*, if we aren't getting anywhere ...'

'You mean we aren't getting where you want to go. However, I understand your frustration. It seems too easy to have Murad be guilty. He is though, more than you know.'

She paused, and smoothed her sarong over he knee. 'Well, I'm in here for murder already, aren't I? So, you're right, it was me. I killed her. I jumped in, smothered her, jumped out and went home. You've caught me.' She looked satisfied with her confession.

'Well now, *Kakak*, that wasn't so hard, was it? You've got your murderer.' And to Osman: 'Can I have a few packs of your cigarettes to take back with me? I'd be grateful.'

Osman opened his mouth to say something, but nothing came out. Hamidah stood up. 'Thank you all for coming,' she said, going to each one to formally shake hands. 'I enjoyed our talk, but now, I think I'd like to go and lie down. Don't forget the cigarettes, please! Would it be too rude, do you think, if I asked you to give me the cigarettes you have with you now? You must think I've totally lost my manners here. I haven't, really, but I want them!'

With a bright smile, she stood in front of Osman, her hands outstretched to receive the bounty, and he gave her the two packs he had with him.

After she left them, they sat in silence. 'I can't understand how we have so many confessions and still aren't sure about the murderer.' Maryam was bemused. 'Soon, people who weren't even there will start confessing.'

'I've never seen anything like it,' Osman commented.

'You haven't been on the job that long,' Rubiah reminded him. 'Maybe that's why.'

Maryam sat silent, smoking. She dared not ask for tea or coffee; whatever they had here would be undrinkable, she was sure of it.

'You know,' she finally said after several minutes, 'she thinks Kamal did it. And she's protecting him. She's right, she's already killed Murad, so what's one more murder charge to her?'

'So? Isn't it possible she did it?' Osman asked.

Maryam conceded it was. 'It's possible Murad did it too. But she'll do anything to protect her son. Do we let her?'

'But, Yam,' Rubiah protested, 'we came here thinking it would be her, and now she's said it was. Why have you changed your mind about it?' Rubiah would have been happy with Murad, but she was ready to accept Hamidah. Why look further?

Maryam struggled to explain. 'I thought she'd deny it, but I could see in her eyes when she decided to admit to it that she calculated what her confession would be worth. So, I thought, it isn't so much a confession, but a strategy, and why is that? Because she's protecting someone else.'

Chapter XXXII

Sometime after midnight, a commotion in the *kampong* cracked the silence. There was screaming for help and incoherent shouting. Mamat woke immediately, but Maryam's dreams incorporated the sounds, which became more like nightmares.

While the sounds were louder, they didn't get closer, but other voices cried out, and there were men calling to each other. Mamat ran out through the yard and down the path, squinting to see in the darkness. Three men were wrestling someone to the ground – it looked like an indeterminate blur of arms and legs, all flailing.

One man, suddenly recognizable as a neighbour, leapt away with black liquid streaming down his arm, and the man on the bottom was somehow now free again, running like a drunk, out of balance, without direction. With his eyes adjusting to the night, he recognized Aziz, wielding a *keris,* a wavy-bladed dagger. It was the traditional Malay weapon, but was rarely used anymore; it must have been in his family for years. He was shouting, but Mamat could not make out what exactly, and he realized with a start that the black liquid was blood in the moonlight. Aziz was *amok*!

Maryam came running up behind him and gasped. Both Zainab and Zaiton lay on the ground, unmoving and bloody. Several women were trying to get to them, but Aziz careened around the clearing, ready to kill anyone who came forward. The men tried to corner him, as they would an angry buffalo, careful not to get too close. He was wild-eyed yet unseeing; in the grip of a frenzy. He whirled towards Mamat and Maryam. Mamat stepped back, hoping to draw him in where someone else could grab him from behind.

Dancing back, Aziz followed him, then sliced through the air with his *keris*, nicking Mamat slightly. With a cry, Maryam moved towards him, and Aziz plunged the *keris* into her shoulder, burying up to the hilt. She screamed and fell, and Aziz grabbed another woman and stabbed her in the arm. He then stood suddenly still, turned the *keris* toward himself and fell on it.

The *kampong* was in chaos. The ground seemed muddy with blood, and the wounded lay where they fell. Osman arrived with three cars and the ambulance. It looked like a war zone, with dazed survivors wandering around, and others tending to the wounded. He saw Mamat with a clean sarong wrapped around his arm, and hailed him. 'What happened?' He could not take in the scene before him.

'Maryam,' Mamat half sobbed, pointing down at her. Osman called for the doctor to come over immediately and get her to the hospital.

'It's my fault,' the police chief moaned. 'I never should have asked her ...'

Mamat, who at any other time would have comforted him

and told him not to feel guilty, sat in shocked silence, as though insensible to all else going on around him.

Rubiah and her family had come out, as had almost everyone in the village, to help those hurt and try to save them. Both Zainab and Zaiton were hurried off to the hospital, with great concern about their condition.

'How are they?' Osman asked anxiously. The doctor merely shook his head sadly, and went to care for others, hurt but still conscious. 'Why did he do it?' he asked Mamat, but once again, Mamat sat silent and unmoving.

Maryam had been stitched up, the wound in her shoulder deep and painful, but thankfully, not affecting her vital organs. She was pale, and frightened, and relieved to find herself alive at the hospital rather than dead on the ground in Kampong Penambang. She still could not clearly make out what had occurred, or why, though Rubiah sat with her and tried to clarify it.

'He was *amok*,' she told her while plumping the pillows and wiping her face with a cold cloth. 'I don't know what pushed him.'

'Guilt, shame,' Maryam listed smartly. 'He thinks Zaiton killed her mother, he attacked me, it's all too much for him. And *Pak* Nik Lah did say he could do this.'

'But he didn't think it would actually happen.'

Maryam could not shrug, but made an eloquent face which was just as expressive. 'These are things you can never know for sure,' she said with a certainly she could not possibly possess. However, in the past several hours she found herself a newly minted expert on the syndrome of *amok*, from a much more intimate perspective than she had ever wanted. 'I imagine he'd been brooding (remember how dangerous that can be!) and decided he couldn't take it anymore. What about his girls?'

Rubiah sighed. 'I don't know yet. They lost such a lot of blood, Yam. They didn't look real anymore, so white. Lying there, it seemed they had no blood left.'

Maryam nearly burst into tears. 'I saw. I don't know about the baby, how it could survive something like this …' She plucked at the sheet covering her. 'Tell me,' she said slowly, fearing the answer, 'Were Zainab's children there?'

'No, *Alhamdulillah*,' Rubiah said thankfully. 'Zainab was just visiting. The kids were home with their father.'

'So she's not divorced yet?'

Rubiah shook her head. 'No, it doesn't look like that's going to happen. Good for her husband, I say. He's doing the right thing.'

Maryam nodded. 'And Zaiton's husband?'

Rubiah shook her head. 'No sign of him. Not that I'm surprised. He's gone, that's all.'

'Is she …?'

'I don't know. But it can't be good for the baby, her losing that much blood. Even if she's alright.'

'I wonder why he isn't coming back?'

'He's a coward,' Rubiah sniffed. 'And to think I thought he was such a nice boy.'

'Not anymore?'

'Nice boys don't leave their wives in this kind of situation. Look what's happened in the end. I know,' she held up her hand to forestall any comments. 'No one knew Aziz was about to snap. But a husband shouldn't just leave his wife like that.'

'Unless he had a reason.'

'What kind of reason? How can you justify it?'

'I don't know. Maybe I'm confused.'

'You certainly have a right to be!' Rubiah declared. 'Maybe you need to rest.'

'I don't know,' Maryam said fretfully. She turned to her side, wincing. 'It hurts when I move.'

'No surprise about that. Look what you've just survived.'

'Wake me when you find out how the others are.' And almost as soon as she closed her eyes, she was asleep.

The hallway of Kota Bharu General Hospital had become a makeshift triage staging point and pandemonium reigned. Osman tried to cut through the crowd and reach the doctor in charge to get some kind of report. He found him in the emergency room, stitching up the neighbour who had first been stabbed. 'You'll be alright,' he assured him tiredly. He turned to give the nurse some instructions, then turned and found Osman.

'The police, right?'

Osman nodded. 'What's the summary here?'

The doctor blotted his forehead with his sleeve. 'It's unbelievable. I've never seen anything like it. Let's see, I have a middle-aged woman admitted, with wounds in the shoulder and arm. She's got stitches, but seems stable.' That would be Maryam, Osman guessed.

'I have a young woman with a blood transfusion, she's lost a lot and I don't know the prognosis. Her husband is in with her. I can't even operate until she stabilizes.' Zainab.

'Two other women with cuts to the arm; the wounds have been closed, they'll be alright. A man admitted, nasty cut to the arm, just missed killing him. He's getting blood, and I think, I hope, he'll be alright. The man with the *keris*? He killed himself. Fell on it. He's dead.' The doctor was silent.

'And one young woman lost too much blood, she died a few minutes ago, poor thing. Never regained consciousness.' He shook his head slowly.

'Zaiton?' Osman asked with a slight quaver in his voice.

He shrugged. 'I don't remember her name. She's in there,' he pointed to a room at the end of the hallway.

Osman took the long walk down the corridor, not wanting to find what was at the end. Rahman joined him on the march. 'Any dead?' he asked.

Osman nodded, suddenly too dejected to speak, and Rahman maintained a discreet silence. In the room were the two bodies, father and daughter. Zaiton looked like a wax doll, so white and bloodless.

Osman stood over her, and began to cry, making no noise, tears falling out of his eyes. Such a waste of two lives, both so very young. It was more than he could bear. Rahman stood quietly next to him, a solid presence. 'What drove him to it?' he finally asked, but Rahman had no answers.

* * *

After several days, the uproar died down. Injured villagers returned to their homes, wounds began to heal, the first, overwhelming shock of the disaster ebbed, leaving Kampong Penambang to interpret what had happened, able to consider it now rather than freezing into immobility.

Maryam was back at the market, unable to move her arm, but comforted by the noise and the bustle which formed the background to her daily life. Ashikin sat next to her, with Nuraini on her lap, helping show the fabrics and keeping her mother occupied with the baby.

'Isn't it fun coming to work?' she cooed to her grandchild, passing her a stream of snacks and stuffed toys to keep her smiling. 'Are you happy here?'

Nuraini's shrieks of glee made clear she was. Customers stopped by and smiled at the three generations manning the stall, and could not resist chucking the baby under the chin while they were there. And then, of course, buying something. Maryam sighed with contentment: life got no better than this, and furthermore, lunch was to be delivered right to the stall!

Osman, however, had not been able to fall back into a comforting routine, though Azrina tried her best. She urged him to declare the case closed – three of his suspects were dead, and it appeared that everyone involved with the case had lost the impetus to continue digging. 'Please, *Abang*,' she implored him. 'I think everyone's been through enough. One of them must have done it!'

He looked at her with exhausted eyes which sleep itself did not seem to cure. 'That isn't how I look at it,' he tried to articulate why he was so unsatisfied. 'I want the person who was actually guilty.'

'Have you spoken to *Mak Cik* Maryam about it?'

He shook his head. 'I can't bother her right now. It isn't fair.' With that, if nothing else, Azrina agreed.

And then a call arrived: a policeman at the tiny station near Semut Api contacted Osman on the crackly phone line, clearly excited about having vital information to be passed on to headquarters.

'Chief Osman?'

'Yes,' he answered slowly.

'Zainal Abidin here, from Pantai Cinta Berahi police.'

'Yes?'

'I thought you would like to know ... (here crackling intervened) ... came back from Thailand. He's here now!'

'Who?' Osman felt a spark of excitement.

'Rahim! He's back from Thailand, staying with his parents.'

'Really? I'll be right out. Make sure he doesn't go anywhere!'

'Will do!' Zainal Abidin said smartly. Osman could almost hear him salute over the phone.

Chapter XXXIII

'Where have you been?' Osman demanded.

Rahim hung his head and looked abashed. 'Thailand,' he mumbled.

The two of them sat in the only chairs in the small police *pondok,* or hut, on the beach. Rahman and Zainal Abidin were lounging outside on a bench, drinking iced tea and swapping stories of the force. Every policeman in Kelantan had heard about Rahman's capture of the murder suspect at the Kota Bharu market, and his subsequent injuries, and Rahman was not adverse to retelling the tale yet again.

'Well, you certainly haven't helped your wife much, have you? You just left her here to fend for herself? Do you know what happened to her?' As Rahim sat there dumb, as Osman grew more angry.

'She confessed to killing her own mother,' Osman continued. 'Can you imagine how confused and guilty she must have been? And you were in Thailand,' he said witheringly. 'Too embarrassed to help her.'

Rahim seemed to have turned to stone, unable to move or

think. Finally he squawked, 'She confessed to you?'

'Yes, she did,' Osman assured him. 'Before she died.'

Rahim stared at him.

'You knew she was dead, didn't you?'

'I just heard. That's why I came back.'

'It's a pity you didn't come back earlier, when you could have helped her.'

'But I was thinking of going back,' he said, slowly. 'I mean, the baby and everything ...'

'When was the last time you spoke to her?'

Rahim stared at him, apparently unable to understand the question. Osman prodded him.

'Not since I left.'

'But you knew she confessed.'

Rahim nodded, still looking surpised.

'Why did you leave?' Osman was growing more furious with each question and halting answer, and he could not really explain why. It seemed that all his wrath and fear were focused on Rahim; someone had to be at fault for all that had happened. He knew it wasn't fair, but was unable to control it.

'My parents thought I should.' Rahim now looked uncomfortable. 'They heard she'd confessed, and thought if she killed her mother, then who else wouldn't she kill?'

'Is that fair?' Rahman interjected, he and Zainal Abidin having listened at the door. 'I mean, do you think she did it?'

'She said she did.'

'Did she talk to you about it?' Rahman took over the questioning, as Osman looked ominously as though he might explode.

'She did the night before. She told me then.'

'And you said ...'

'What could I say?' Rahim protested. 'I was shocked, surprised, I didn't know what to say. "You killed your mother?"'

'Did she mean to, do you think?'

'Kill her? I don't know.'

Osman abruptly jumped back into the interrogation. 'Rahim, that isn't an answer. Perhaps it would be best if you come back to Kota Bharu with us. We can talk more easily there.'

'Wait a minute! My parents ...'

'They can come too,' Osman fairly spit. It would be much better to have Maryam talk to him, he was too angry to get anything done.

But the station in Kota Bharu was crowded and loud. Rahim's mother protested loudly that her son had been dragged – yes, dragged! – from his home in Semut Api all the way to Kota Bharu for no reason. No reason at all! Even the cups of coffee provided to her did not lower the volume.

Rahim sat at the table, lighting one cigarette from the butt of the last, his coffee cooling in front of him. Zainal Abidin wandered around the office, asking about everything, exclaiming in delight at the equipment available.

And finally, Maryam and Rubiah came in, taken from the market against their will, part resigned, part sulky, prepared with their own cache of cakes. They both gave Osman disgusted looks as he held the door open for them to come into the room. Even with the door closed, the hum of noise still penetrated, though it was not as piercing as it had been with the door open.

'He just came back from Thailand,' Osman explained to them.

'Why?' Maryam asked.

It took Rahim a moment to realize he was supposed to answer. 'Oh! I heard what happened.'

Maryam looked at him, saying nothing.

'You know, about Aziz becoming *amok*.' He gestured towards her arm. 'I see you were hurt ...'

'Oh yes,' Maryam agreed. 'I was.'

He gulped.

'So, you came back here when you heard Zaiton had died?'

He was silent, as though he didn't realize anyone was speaking to him.

'Rahim!' Maryam ordered in her most military voice. 'Answer me!'

'Oh. Yes, when I heard she had ... died.'

'And the child, too, of course.' As soon as she said it, she berated herself for meanness. Was that really necessary?

He sat stone-faced.

'And Aziz and Jamillah,' she continued inexorably. 'Except for Zainab, who lost so much blood she's still in the hospital, nearly the whole family is gone. What a tragedy.'

He mumbled something unintelligible.

'What?' she prompted him.

She realized he was talking to himself, not paying any attention to her. She waited. Whatever he was doing, he needed to finish this discussion with himself before she could continue questioning him. She was becoming impatient, but knew that interrupting would just drag out the process, and she was interested in learning how this argument would end.

He drew his sleeve over his forehead and covered his eyes with his hands. 'I can't,' he said clearly, and shook his head. He looked up at her, rose from his chair, and paced the length of the table. 'I just can't,' he repeated, louder this time. Then he sat down.

It seemed he had come to a decision. He looked at Maryam and then at Osman. He put his hands flat on his knees and bent over. 'Alright. I'll tell you.'

They waited silently.

'I did it.' He was rocking back and forth. 'I did it, and I let Zaiton confess to it and probably drove her father to *amok*, and I knew the truth all the time but didn't say anything.'

It was now Maryam's turn to stare. Rahim was moaning softly. 'I should have stopped her, I know, but I couldn't think of any way to do it except to tell her it was me who did it, and I was afraid. So I let her confess and went home, and listened to my parents tell me to leave her because she killed her own mother. But it was me.'

'And we thought you were so nice,' Maryam said with a note of disillusion. And then she thought about what she'd said. 'You're a good liar,' she continued. 'Very cool, you didn't flinch when we were questioning you.'

'I know. I just didn't think about it.'

'There are people who would have trouble doing that.' She paused. 'Tell me what happened.'

He rubbed his hands on his sarong, as if to clean them. He sighed. He asked for coffee, for cigarettes. 'Tell me,' she ordered him again.

He lit his cigarette and stared at the floor. 'Zaiton thought her mother would come around to let us marry,' he began, his face smoothing out as he spoke, as though the very act of unburdening himself would ease his conscience.

'I knew she wouldn't. I'd had a talk with her, you see, the day before the *main puteri*. My family had already gone to ask for Zaiton, but her parents were very vague, very non-committal, and my father noticed it right away. He said it was no use, they wouldn't agree.

'So I thought, maybe if I talk to *Mak Cik* Jamillah and tell her how hard I would try to be a good husband, she'd change her mind. She was the one against it, you see, not *Pak Cik* Aziz.

'So I spoke to her. She wasn't feeling very well, I knew that, but after all, Zaiton was having a baby and we didn't have lots of time. I told Zaiton to tell her mother she was pregnant – that would change her mind for sure. But she wouldn't.'

Rahim shook his head. 'She wouldn't do it. She was afraid to tell her parents, and was hoping to get married without anyone finding out.

'So, when I went to speak to *Mak Cik* Jamillah, she didn't know, so she didn't understand why I was so anxious. She tried to be nice about it, and said she didn't think I was ready yet to support a wife. A polite way of saying I was too poor, I suppose. Maybe if I worked hard and made something of myself, she said, we could marry then.

'Well, even if we had time for that, Zaiton would be long married to someone else by that time. I told her then. About the pregnancy. I did.'

He looked up at them, to gauge their reaction. Maryam identified with the mother; how would she feel if Daud had told her that about Ashikin? She'd be livid, and she imagined that was just what they were going to hear now about Jamillah.

'She was furious!' Rahim continued, validating Maryam's surmise. 'I thought she'd kill me. Really. She threw me out of the house.

'Before the *main puteri* started, she said something to Zaiton like "We have a lot to talk about", or something like that. Zaiton told me to meet her at the house when it was all over, and we'd talk to her together. I didn't tell her about my conversation with her mother. Plenty of time for that, I thought.

'So, after the ceremony, Zaiton was putting her mother to bed, and she leaned out the window and called me to come in. I did ...'

'Through the window?' Osman asked.

Rahim nodded. He seemed to enjoy his recitation. '*Mak Cik* Jamillah was really tired. I could see that. She told us, 'I don't have the energy right now. We can do this tomorrow.'

'And Zaiton said, "Why can't you just agree now? Why are you being so difficult?" Her mother just looked at her, and told her that she knew she was pregnant, and she was ashamed, and she wouldn't decide anything now. And she lay down, you see, and Zaiton lost her temper. I think she fell asleep in a second, like that!' He clapped his hands, and lit another cigarette.

'Zaiton just stood there, wringing her hands. "She'll never say yes!" she kept saying. I told her "Don't worry. She has to. We're having a baby! Just wait."

'But no, she just kept moaning about how her life would be ruined now. But really, *Mak Cik*,' he asked Maryam directly, 'what mother is going to stand in the way of her daughter marrying if she's already having a baby? It doesn't make any sense.'

Maryam had to agree. 'Is that why you did it? Got pregnant, I mean.'

Rahim blushed. 'No, it was a mistake. It never should have happened,'

'But if it hadn't, you wouldn't have been able to marry her, you know.'

He shrugged. 'Anyway, Zaiton got more upset, and finally pushed her mother to wake her up, but she was too deep in sleep for that, and she rolled over on her face. 'Leave her there,' Zaiton said. Then she had to go back into the living room with all the relatives. I stood there, ready to leave, and then suddenly, I thought, maybe I can get rid of all the problems about getting married. If *Mak Cik* Jamillah were gone, it would go smoothly. *Pak Cik* Aziz would agree, we'd get married and no more arguments. I wouldn't have to worry about the next day and how she would scold both of us and maybe scold my parents as well. Just like that, it seemed like a good idea and the perfect time to do it. Who would know? No one.

'I don't know what came over me, *Mak Cik*, I really don't. I just rolled her over again to face the wall and held the pillow over her face. She didn't struggle much. I held her neck to do it faster.

Then I put the pillow back on the bed and went out the window.'

'And you never told Zaiton.'

'No. You know, afterward it seemed like a dream, like I didn't really do it. It only took a minute, someone else's minute. Maybe I should have told her so she wouldn't blame herself. But I thought she'd be angry at me.'

'Angry at you? I should think so!' Maryam could hardly believe he worried about that after committing murder. 'You weren't afraid to kill her mother, but you were afraid she'd be angry at you.'

'I guess,' he said lamely. 'I just wanted things to go smoothly.'

Chapter XXXIV

Osman and Azrina came to the house, to find the rare sight of Maryam and Rubiah lounging around on the porch, smoking cigarettes and drinking *teh beng*, iced tea with sweetened condensed milk, congratulating each other on the end of the case.

'*Mak Cik*!' Azrina cried as she mounted the stairs, Osman trailing behind her. 'You really found the killer!'

Maryam was modest, dismissing it as though it was the kind of thing she regularly managed every week. 'But how are you?' Maryam asked.

They sat down on the porch, and Osman passed out cigarettes. Maryam lazily called for Yi and ordered him to get more *teh beng* from the stall close by and to bring out the tray of cakes. 'Ordinarily, I wouldn't do this,' she apologized.

'But we're taking the day off,' Rubiah explained. 'After the case and all.'

'Of course! I hate troubling you ...' Azrina began.

'Not at all,' Maryam said grandly.

'Eat!' Commanded Rubiah with a significant look towards Osman. He began explaining the nature of each cake under

Rubiah's watchful eye.

'You must have eaten quite a few of these,' his wife said, 'to know so much about them.'

'We try,' Rubiah told her. 'He's so skinny.'

Maryam nodded. 'We try to feed him whenever we can.'

'Cakes aren't enough to live on though,' Rubiah said. 'I mean, you can make a meal out of them ...'

'And he has,' Maryam added. 'But it isn't enough. But now that you're here, you can take care of him!'

Azrina smiled at Osman and nodded. 'You know, *Mak Cik*,' she said, leaning in closer, 'my husband told me about Rahim confessing. Who would have thought?'

'I never suspected him. Did you?' Rubiah asked Osman.

'Not really,' Osman admitted. He turned to Maryam. 'But you did.'

She shook her head. 'Not as much as I should have. I was blinded by his manners, and because there were other people so ... crazy!'

Osman nodded. 'But it was you who kept the case open. I think I would have taken Hamidah's word for it if you had agreed.'

Maryam leaned back against the wall, taking a deep drag of the cigarette. 'I thought – that is, I still think – Hamidah may have told Kamal to kill Jamillah, but he was reluctant. That's why she came to Kampong Penambang to do it herself. Well, Kamal isn't as mean as either of his parents, but after a few years with his wife, who knows?'

'Will they stay married, do you think?' Azrina asked.

Maryam shrugged. 'I don't know if his mother-in-law will

want him now that the family is so notorious and he's in jail. We'll see how devoted she is to family.'

'But *Mak Cik*,' Osman pursued, 'why didn't you think she did it?'

'Oh, I thought she would have, no question. She killed her own husband practically with her bare hands!'

'But what a husband,' Rubiah interjected. 'I can understand that.'

'I believed Kamal when he said he found Jamillah already cold. That eliminated Hamidah and Kamal. Murad was mean, but he didn't care enough to kill her. I think he would have killed if it suited him, but Jamillah was no threat, so why?' They all nodded.

'That meant it had to be her family, someone in the house who no one would question. It could well have been Zaiton. I mean, she spent time alone with her mother putting her to sleep, and surely she wouldn't look suspicious at all. But a daughter killing her mother? I'm not saying it couldn't happen, just that I didn't want to believe it.

'It's wrong to look at a crime in that way, I know, but what an awful thing that would be. No, I couldn't think about that. Then it was either Aziz or Rahim. Aziz had no reason at all. So by default, it was Rahim. But I didn't get to that fast enough to save Zaiton.'

'You tried, *Mak Cik*,' Azrina objected. 'You asked to have her released.'

'I couldn't produce the actual killer. Not then. But I wonder if Zaiton would have been any better off if she knew it had been

Rahim. She was heartbroken either way, poor thing.'

'He should have stayed with her.'

'He should have left her mother alone! It was silly! Really, what choice did Jamillah have with Zaiton already pregnant? Of course, she would have agreed to their marriage, after making them suffer a bit. There was absolutely no need to kill her as though she was standing in their way and would never budge. It was a waste of life, and look what it led to? How many people died because of it?'

Maryam willed herself to calm down. This was, she reminded herself, her day off. 'And even those who survived, like me, like Aliza, look what happened here. No, in the end, he was the devil himself with good manners.' She looked morose.

'Are you still interested in crime, then?' Rubiah asked Azrina. She blushed and looked down for a moment, and then looked up with a mischievous grin. 'I must admit, I am. Though it's a lot harder to deal with in real life than it is in books. I can always guess the killer there, but this time, I really had no idea.'

'It's your first time,' Maryam said kindly. 'Just wait till you get some practice.' She took another sip of her tea. 'But it's dangerous. I think I'm getting too old for it. Maybe you should take over – helping Osman, I mean. That way you can work together.'

'How is your Kelantanese coming along?' Rubiah asked, her glasses glinting in the sunlight.

'Well, not so fast. I have to try to make it faster.'

Rubiah nodded. 'It's important. Otherwise, how will you know what people are telling you?' She gave Osman a significant glance.

'And he needs an interpreter,' Maryam added bluntly.

'You'd think by now…' Rubiah began.

'Not now,' Maryam put a hand on her arm. 'This is no time to criticize.'

'You're right,' Rubiah relented. 'You've done a wonderful job.'

Osman tried to smile with a mouthful of cake, but it was difficult.

'I hear you're planning a wedding,' Azrina began. 'Your son?'

Maryam nodded. 'It's my next project.'

'The *songket* will be marvelous, I think.'

'They'll never lack for fabric or fish sauce,' Rubiah told her. 'If they can live on just that, they're set for life.'

Acknowledgements

My grateful thanks to Shahmim Dhilawala, Puteh Shaharizan Shaari and Ashikin Mohd Ali Flindall for their insightful comments on Malay custom. Doug Raybeck, who first introduced me to Kelantan, taught me Malay in college and offered valuable help, not the least of which was his analysis of Main Puteri and its meaning in Kelantanese society. Bonnie Tessler constructed my website, Valerie Vogel read my books with enthusiasm, and Esther Kirk, Michele Bowen and Bryn Barnard read tirelessly, draft after draft. Joanne Spicehandler encouraged me, Richard Lord, my excellent editor, worked wonders on the text, and Phil Tatham believed in the series.

Thank you all!

Kain Songket Mysteries

S

Shadow Play is the first eries set in
the northern state of Ke . Mak Cik
Maryam, a *kain songke* al Market,
discovers a murder in he bucolic
village world she thoug Chief of
Police, a pleasant young monitions
about the wiles of Kelan stles with
the bewildering local dia e mystery
herself. Her investigatio ld of the
wayang kulit shadow pla rmers—a
world riven by rivalries tangle of
jealousy, Maryam strugg spite of
the spells sent to keep her voven to
shield the guilty.

PRI

Mak Cik Maryam is plu y world
of murder, hatred and m woman is
killed after a successful *main puteri* (princess play) curing ceremony. Suddenly, the villagers she thought she knew reveal secrets she never suspected, while her good sense and solid courage lead her to unmask the murderer among them. Follow Maryam in *Princess Play*, the second Kelantanese murder case in the Kain Songket Mysteries series.

Songbird (Vol.3)

Singing doves appear to be the gentlest of creatures, and songbird contests among the most refined and rarified of activities in the northern state of Kelantan, Malaysia. Yet passions run deep among the competitors, and a shocking murder stuns the community. Mak Cik Maryam must find the murderer before more innocent lives are lost. Her investigations take her throughout Kelantan, as she guides the police in the not particularly gentle way they have come to appreciate. Join Maryam in her latest adventure, *Songbird*, the third installment in the Kain Songket Mysteries series.